# 序 言

　　這本「初級英語寫作口說測驗」，是專門為參加全民英語能力分級檢定「初級英語檢定測驗」的讀者而編寫的。本書的內容是針對「初級英語檢定測驗」第二階段的複試測驗。

　　許多人通過了「初級英語檢定測驗」初試，但是，對於即將面臨的複試，心存不安，因為「初級英語檢定測驗」複試中，**寫作能力測驗**無法憑運氣得分，需靠紮實的英文書寫能力。而**口說能力測驗**本來就是台灣學生較弱的一環，學了英文，卻不會說。

　　本書共有八回，每一回都是一個完整的測驗，提供讀者各種可能的出題模式，讓題型更臻完整。寫作部份我們將「初檢」範圍內的文法，融入試題當中，讀者研讀本書，可熟悉考試的模式，也可藉由書中的文法解說，加強文法觀念；口說部份由專業的美籍播音員錄製，讀者可跟著練習，模仿他們的語調及發音，說起英文來，就會像道地的美國人。

　　本書在編審及校對的每一階段，均力求完善，但恐有疏漏之處，誠盼各界先進不吝批評指正。

劉　毅

# 初級英語檢定測驗第二階段

# 寫作口說能力測驗①

## 寫作能力測驗

本測驗共有兩部份。第一部份為單句寫作，第二部份為段落寫作。測驗時間為 40 分鐘。

### 第一部份：單句寫作

請將答案寫在答案紙上對應的題號旁，如有文法、用字、拼字、標點符號、大小寫等之錯誤，將予扣分。

### 第 1～5 題：句子改寫

請依題目之提示，將原句依指定型式改寫，並將改寫的句子<u>完整</u>地寫在答案紙上。

注意：須寫出提示之文字及標點符號。

例： 題目：I am fine.

　　　　She ＿＿＿＿＿＿＿.

在答案紙上寫：***She is fine.***

1. I often play tennis.

   I ＿＿＿＿＿＿＿＿＿＿＿＿＿＿ when you called me.

2. Someone ate the last cookie.

   Who ＿＿＿＿＿＿＿＿＿＿＿＿＿＿＿?

3. The movie starts at 3:00.

What time _____?

4. Where is the stationery store?

Tell me _____.

5. I made a cake for my mother.

I made my mother _____.

第 6~10 題：句子合併

　　請依照題目指示，將兩句合併成一句。並將合併的句子完整地寫在答案紙上。

　　注意：須寫出提示之文字及標點符號。

例：題目：John has a cap.

　　　　　The cap is purple.

　　　　　John _____ cap.

　　在答案紙上寫：***John has a purple cap.***

6. It is raining.

We can't go to the park.

_____ because _____.

7. I was reading the book.

The book is on the table.

I _____ that _____.

8. I will do my homework.

   Then I will watch TV.

   I _____ after _____.

9. I was playing the piano.

   My sister was cleaning her room.

   I _____ while _____.

10. I washed the dishes.

    I didn't wash the clothes.

    I _____, but _____.

第 11～15 題：重組

　　請將題目中所有提示的字詞整合成一有意義的句子，並將重組的
　　句子完整地寫在答案紙上。

　　注意： 須寫出提示之文字及標點符號。( 答案中必須使用所有提
　　　　　示的字詞，且不能隨意增減字詞，否則不予計分。 )

例： 題目：John _____.

　　　　　this morning / late / was / again

　　在答案紙上寫：***John was late again this morning.***

11. I _____.

    the first time / to / went / the store / for / yesterday

12. It _____.

the lake / too / was / go swimming / cold / to / in

13. I'm _____.

my friends / the mall / to / going / on Saturday / with / to go

14. I _____.

because / time / didn't take a nap / I / today / didn't have

15. Who _____?

near / girl / the door / is / beautiful / standing / that

## 第二部份：段落寫作

題目：昨天南西（Nancy）幫她的鄰居照顧小孩，但是小孩不
停地在哭鬧，南西試著哄小孩。請根據圖片內容寫一篇
約 50 字的簡短描述。

# 口說能力測驗

*請在 15 秒內完成並唸出下列自我介紹的句子,請開始:

My seat number is (複試座位號碼) , and my test number is (初試准考證號碼) .

## I. 複誦

共五題。題目不印在試題上,由耳機播出,每題播出兩次,兩次之間大約有一到二秒的間隔。聽完兩次後,請馬上複誦一次。

## II. 朗讀句子與短文

共有五個句子及一篇短文,請先利用一分鐘的時間閱讀試題上的句子與短文,然後在一分鐘內以正常的速度,清楚正確的朗讀一遍。

One　: I didn't know that the store was closed.

Two　: The children played outside until they were tired.

Three : Luckily, we won the game in the end.

Four　: You brought the book, didn't you?

Five　: This is your table.

Six : I wanted to buy a birthday gift for my sister.
I planned to buy her a bottle of her favorite
perfume. I went to the department store to
buy it. I was shocked by how expensive it
was! I really couldn't afford it. So I got her
a nice book instead. I hope she likes it.

## III. 回答問題

共七題。題目不印在試題上，由耳機播出，每題播出兩次，兩
次之間大約有一到二秒的間隔。聽完兩次後，請馬上回答，每
題回答時間為 15 秒，請在作答時間內儘量的表達。

* 請將下列自我介紹的句子再唸一遍，請開始：

My seat number is （複試座位號碼）, and my test number is
（初試准考證號碼）.

# 寫作口說能力測驗 ① 詳解

## 寫作能力測驗詳解

### 第一部份：單句寫作

**第 1～5 題：句子改寫**

1. I often play tennis.

   I _____ when you called me.

   > **重點結構：** 過去進行式
   >
   > 　**解　答：** I was playing tennis when you called me.
   >
   > **句型分析：** 主詞＋動詞（過去進行式）＋when＋主詞＋
   > 　　　　　　　動詞（過去式）
   >
   > 　**說　明：** 本句的意思是「當你打電話給我的時候，我正在打
   > 　　　　　　網球」，指在過去某一特定的時刻，某動作正在進行
   > 　　　　　　中，因此主要句子 I often play tennis 應改成過去
   > 　　　　　　進行式的用法，即「be 動詞過去式＋現在分詞」。
   >
   > 　＊ play〔ple〕v. 打（球）　　　tennis〔'tɛnɪs〕n. 網球
   > 　　call〔kɔl〕v. 給電話給

2. Someone ate the last cookie.

   Who _____?

   > **重點結構：** 直述句改為疑問句
   >
   > 　**解　答：** Who ate the last cookie?

句型分析：Who + 動詞（過去式）+ 受詞？

説　明：疑問詞 Who 在此爲疑問代名詞，做主詞來用，故後面不須加助動詞，並把句號改成問號，形成問句。

\* someone (ˈsʌmˌwʌn ) *pron.* 某人　　***the last*** 最後的
cookie (ˈkʊkɪ ) *n.* 餅乾

3. The movie starts at 3:00.
   What time _____?

重點結構：直述句改爲疑問句

解　答：<u>What time does the movie start?</u>

句型分析：What time + 助動詞 + 主詞 + 動詞？

説　明：直述句改成 What time（何時）的疑問句，須用助動詞 do 或 does，主詞 the movie 爲單數，故用助動詞 does，並與主詞 the movie 倒裝，助動詞後的動詞須用原形動詞，故 starts 改成 start，並把句號改成問號。

\* movie (ˈmuvɪ ) *n.* 電影　　start ( stɑrt ) *v.* 開始

4. Where is the stationery store?
   Tell me _____.

重點結構：直接問句改爲間接問句

解　答：<u>Tell me where the stationery store is.</u>

句型分析：Tell me + where + 主詞 + 動詞

説　明：Tell me 後面須接受詞，故直接問句 Where is the stationery store? 須改爲間接問句當受詞，即「疑問詞 + 主詞 + 動詞」的形式，並把問號改成句點。

\* stationery (ˈsteʃənˌɛrɪ ) *n.* 文具　　***stationery store*** 文具店

5. I made a cake for my mother.

   I made my mother ＿＿＿＿＿＿＿＿＿＿＿＿＿＿＿＿＿.

   　重點結構：make 做授與動詞的用法

   　　解　答：<u>I made my mother a cake.</u>

   　句型分析：主詞 + make + 直接受詞（人）+ 間接受詞（物）

   　　說　明：這題的意思是「我幫我媽媽做了一個蛋糕」，有兩種
   　　　　　　寫法：「make + sb. + sth.」或「make + sth. + for
   　　　　　　+ sb.」，這題要改成第一種寫法，先寫人（my
   　　　　　　mother），再寫物（a cake）。

   　　* cake〔kek〕n. 蛋糕

第 6～10 題：句子合併

6. It is raining.

   We can't go to the park.

   ＿＿＿＿＿＿＿＿＿ because ＿＿＿＿＿＿＿＿＿＿＿.

   　重點結構：because 的用法

   　　解　答：<u>We can't go to the park because it is raining.</u>

   　句型分析：主詞 + 動詞 + because + 主詞 + 動詞

   　　說　明：連接詞 because（因為）引導副詞子句，後面接原
   　　　　　　因，按照句意，「我們不能去公園，因為下雨了」，
   　　　　　　因此先寫 We can't go to the park，再寫 it is
   　　　　　　raining。

   　　* rain〔ren〕v. 下雨　　park〔pɑrk〕n. 公園

7. I was reading the book.

The book is on the table.

I _____ that _____.

    重點結構：that 引導形容詞子句

    解　答：<u>I was reading the book that is on the table.</u>

    句型分析：主詞＋動詞＋受詞＋that＋動詞

    說　明：that 在此為關係代名詞，引導形容詞子句，修飾先行詞 the book，而在形容詞子句中，that 亦代替先行詞做為主詞，故後面接動詞 is on the table。

    \* read〔rɪd〕*v.* 閱讀　　table〔'tebḷ〕*n.* 桌子

8. I will do my homework.

Then I will watch TV.

I _____ after _____.

    重點結構：after 的用法

    解　答：<u>I will watch TV after I do my homework.</u>

        或 <u>I will watch TV after doing my homework.</u>

    句型分析：主詞＋動詞＋after＋主詞＋動詞

        或 主詞＋動詞＋after＋（動）名詞

    說　明：由副詞 then（然後）可知，我先做功課，再看電視，用 after「在～之後」來表示事情的先後順序。當 after 作為連接詞引導副詞子句時，須接含主詞與動詞的完整子句，即 after I do my homework；若作為介系詞，須接動名詞或名詞，即 after doing my homework。

    \* homework〔'hom,wɝk〕*n.* 功課

9. I was playing the piano.

My sister was cleaning her room.

I ＿＿＿＿＿＿＿＿＿＿＿＿ while ＿＿＿＿＿＿＿＿＿＿＿＿＿＿.

重點結構：while 的用法

解　答：I was playing the piano while my sister was cleaning her room.

句型分析：主詞＋動詞（進行式）＋while＋主詞＋動詞（進行式）

説　明：while（當…時）後面接副詞子句，通常是持續一段時間的動作，故常用進行式；當主要子句也是進行式時，表示某個動作正在進行的同時，另一個動作也在進行中。

* play〔ple〕v. 彈奏　　piano〔pɪˋæno〕n. 鋼琴
　clean〔klin〕v. 打掃　　room〔rum〕n. 房間

10. I washed the dishes.

I didn't wash the clothes.

I ＿＿＿＿＿＿＿＿＿＿＿＿, but ＿＿＿＿＿＿＿＿＿＿＿＿＿＿.

重點結構：but 的用法

解　答：I washed the dishes but I didn't wash the clothes.
　　　　或 I didn't wash the clothes, but I washed the dishes.

句型分析：主詞＋動詞＋but＋主詞＋動詞否定
　　　　或 主詞＋動詞否定＋,＋but＋主詞＋動詞

説　明：but（但是）為「對等連接詞」，可用來連接前後句意相反，但文法功能相同的兩個單字、片語或子句等。

* wash〔waʃ〕v. 洗　　dish〔dɪʃ〕n. 碗盤
　clothes〔kloz〕n. pl. 衣服

第 11～15 題：重組

11. I _____.

the first time / to / went / the store / for / yesterday

> 重點結構：for the first time 的用法
>
> 解　答：I went to the store for the first time yesterday.
>
> 　或 I went to the store yesterday for the first time.
>
> 句型分析：主詞 + 動詞 + for the first time
>
> 說　明：本句的意思是「我昨天第一次去那間店」，for the first time 當副詞用，可放在動詞之後或句尾。
>
> \* store〔stɔr〕*n.* 商店　　***for the first time*** 生平第一次

12. It _____.

the lake / too / was / go swimming / cold / to / in

> 重點結構：「too…to V.」的用法
>
> 解　答：It was too cold to go swimming in the lake.
>
> 句型分析：主詞 + be 動詞 + too + 形容詞 + to V.
>
> 說　明：這題的意思是說「天氣太冷了，沒辦法在湖裡游泳」，It 是指天氣，用「too…to V.」合併兩句，表「太…以致於不～」。
>
> \* cold〔kold〕*adj.* 冷的　　***go swimming*** 去游泳
>
> 　lake〔lek〕*n.* 湖

13. I'm _____.

my friends / the mall / to / going / on Saturday / with / go to

> 重點結構：未來式的用法

解　答：I'm going to go to the mall with my friends on Saturday.

句型分析：主詞 + be going to + 原形動詞 + with + 受詞

說　明：依句意，「我星期六將和我的朋友們去購物中心」，未來式可用「be going to + V.」來表現。

* mall〔mɔl〕n. 購物中心

14. I _____.

because / time / didn't take a nap / I / today / didn't have

重點結構：because 的用法

解　答：I didn't take a nap today because I didn't have time.

句型分析：主詞 + 動詞 + because + 主詞 + 動詞

說　明：連接詞 because（因為）引導副詞子句，後面接原因，按照句意，「我今天沒有午睡，因為我沒時間」。因此先寫結果 I didn't take a nap today，再寫原因 I didn't have time。

* nap〔næp〕n. 小睡；午睡　*take a nap* 小睡片刻；午睡

15. Who _____?

near / girl / the door / is / beautiful / standing / that

重點結構：問句基本結構

解　答：Who is that beautiful girl standing near the door?

句型分析：Who + be 動詞 + 補語 + 形容詞片語？

說　明：這題的意思是「站在門附近的那位漂亮女孩是誰？」
Who 為疑問詞，先找出 be 動詞 is，再接補語 that
beautiful girl，而 standing near the door 作為形
容詞片語，修飾 that beautiful girl。

* beautiful〔'bjutəfəl〕*adj.* 漂亮的　　stand〔stænd〕*v.* 站
near〔nɪr〕*prep.* 在…的附近

## 第二部份：段落寫作

【作文範例】

　　*Yesterday* Nancy was babysitting her neighbor's son.
As soon as his mother left, the boy cried and cried. Nancy
tried to cheer him up. She danced and sang, but the boy still
cried. Finally, Nancy gave him a bottle. The boy hit the
bottle and milk spilled all over Nancy's shirt. Nancy began
to cry. Then the little boy laughed and clapped his hands.

* babysit〔'bebɪ,sɪt〕*v.* 照顧嬰兒；當臨時褓姆
neighbor〔'nebɚ〕*n.* 鄰居　　son〔sʌn〕*n.* 兒子
*as soon as* 一…就～　　leave〔liv〕*v.* 離開
cry〔kraɪ〕*v.* 哭　　try〔traɪ〕*v.* 嘗試
*cheer sb. up* 使某人振作起來　　dance〔dæns〕*v.* 跳舞
sing〔sɪŋ〕*v.* 唱歌　　still〔stɪl〕*adv.* 仍然
finally〔'faɪnlɪ〕*adv.* 最後　　bottle〔'batl〕*n.* 瓶子；奶瓶
hit〔hɪt〕*v.* 打中　　milk〔mɪlk〕*n.* 牛奶
spill〔spɪl〕*v.* 灑出　　*all over* 在…到處
shirt〔ʃɜt〕*n.* 襯衫；上衣　　begin〔bɪ'gɪn〕*v.* 開始
laugh〔læf〕*v.* 笑　　clap〔klæp〕*v.* 拍（手）

# 口說能力測驗詳解

\* 請在 15 秒內完成並唸出下列自我介紹的句子，請開始：

My seat number is （複試座位號碼），and my test number is （初試准考證號碼）.

## I. 複誦

共五題。題目不印在試題上，由耳機播出，每題播出兩次，兩次之間大約有一到二秒的間隔。聽完兩次後，請馬上複誦一次。

1. I had a wonderful time last night. 我昨晚過得很愉快。

2. Don't forget to take out the trash.
   不要忘了把垃圾拿出去。

3. This is my favorite show. 這是我最喜愛的節目。

4. I'd like a cup of tea. 我想要一杯茶。

5. The store is closed. 這家店沒開。

【註】 wonderful〔'wʌndəfəl〕*adj.* 美好的
　　　 forget〔fə'gɛt〕*v.* 忘記　　***take out*** 將…帶出去
　　　 trash〔træʃ〕*n.* 垃圾
　　　 favorite〔'fevərɪt〕*adj.* 最喜愛的
　　　 show〔ʃo〕*n.* 節目；表演
　　　 tea〔ti〕*n.* 茶　　***a cup of tea*** 一杯茶
　　　 store〔stor〕*n.* 商店
　　　 closed〔klozd〕*adj.* 關閉的；停止營業的

## II. 朗讀句子與短文

共有五個句子及一篇短文，請先利用一分鐘的時間閱讀試題上的句子與短文，然後在一分鐘內以正常的速度，清楚正確的朗讀一遍。

One　: I didn't know that the store was closed.
　　　我不知道那家店沒開。

Two　: The children played outside until they were tired.
　　　小孩們在外面玩耍，直到他們累了。

Three : Luckily, we won the game in the end.
　　　幸運的是，我們最後贏得了比賽。

Four　: You brought the book, didn't you?
　　　你把書帶來了，不是嗎？

Five　: This is your table.
　　　這是你的桌子。

【註】 children (ˈtʃɪldrən) n. pl. 小孩　　play ( ple ) v. 玩
　　　outside (ˈaʊtˈsaɪd) adv. 在外面
　　　until ( ənˈtɪl ) conj. 直到…
　　　tired ( taɪrd ) adj. 累的
　　　luckily (ˈlʌkɪlɪ) adv. 幸運地
　　　win ( wɪn ) v. 贏得　　game ( gem ) n. 比賽
　　　end ( ɛnd ) n. 結束；終了　　*in the end* 最後
　　　bring ( brɪŋ ) v. 帶來

Six：I wanted to buy a birthday gift for my sister.
I planned to buy her a bottle of her favorite
perfume.  I went to the department store to
buy it.  I was shocked by how expensive it
was！I really couldn't afford it.  So I got her
a nice book instead.  I hope she likes it.

我想要買送給我姊姊的生日禮物。我計畫買一瓶她
最喜歡的香水。我到百貨公司去買。被香水昂貴的
價格給嚇到！我真的買不起。所以我買了一本好書
給她作為代替。希望她會喜歡。

【註】birthday〔'bɝθ,de〕n. 生日
　　　gift〔gɪft〕n. 禮物　　plan〔plæn〕v. 計畫
　　　bottle〔'batḷ〕n. 瓶　　perfume〔'pɝfjum〕n. 香水
　　　department〔dɪ'partmənt〕n. 部門
　　　*department store* 百貨公司
　　　shocked〔ʃakt〕adj. 震驚的
　　　expensive〔ɪk'spɛnsɪv〕adj. 昂貴的
　　　really〔'rɪəlɪ〕adv. 真地
　　　afford〔ə'ford〕v. 買得起
　　　get〔gɛt〕v. 買　　nice〔naɪs〕adj. 很好的
　　　instead〔ɪn'stɛd〕adv. 作為代替
　　　hope〔hop〕v. 希望　　like〔laɪk〕v. 喜歡

## Ⅲ. 回答問題

共七題。題目不印在試題上，由耳機播出，每題播出兩次，兩次之間大約有一到二秒的間隔。聽完兩次後，請馬上回答，每題回答時間為 15 秒，請在作答時間內儘量的表達。

1. **Q** : Your friend gives you a present on your birthday. What will you say to him or her?

你的朋友在你生日當天給你一個禮物。你會跟他（她）說什麼？

**A1** : I'll say, "Thank you! You're so kind to remember my birthday."

我會說：「謝謝你！你真是體貼，記得我的生日。」

**A2** : I'll say, "Thank you. This really means a lot to me. You made my day."

我會說：「謝謝你。這對我來說意義很大。你讓我今天很開心。」

【註】 present〔'prɛznt〕*n.* 禮物（ = *gift* ）
kind〔kaɪnd〕*adj.* 體貼的
remember〔'rɪmɛmbɚ〕*v.* 記得
mean〔min〕*v.* 具有…重要性　　*a lot* 很多
*mean a lot* 意義重大
*You made my day.* 你讓我今天很開心。

**A3**：I'll say, "You shouldn't have!　You didn't need to get me a gift.　It's so thoughtful of you."
我會說：「你真不該這麼做！你不需要買禮物給我的。你真貼心。」

2. **Q**　：What would you do if you ordered a meal at a restaurant and, when it was served, it was cold?
如果你在餐廳點餐，當菜送來時已經冷掉了，你會怎麼做？

**A1**：I'd call the waiter and say, "Excuse me, but my food is cold.　Please bring me another plate."
我會叫服務生過來，並且說：「不好意思，我的食物是冷的。請你換另一盤給我。」

【註】　*You shouldn't have!* 你真不該這麼做！
need ( nid ) *v.* 需要　　get ( gɛt ) *v.* 買
thoughtful ('θɔtfəl ) *adj.* 體貼的
order ('ɔrdɚ ) *v.* 點（餐）　　meal ( mil ) *n.* 一餐
restaurant ('rɛstərənt ) *n.* 餐廳
serve ( sɜv ) *v.* 將…端上（餐桌）
cold ( kold ) *adj.* 冷的　　call ( kɔl ) *v.* 呼叫
waiter ('wetɚ ) *n.* 服務生
food ( fud ) *n.* 食物
another ( ə'nʌðɚ ) *adj.* 另一的
plate ( plet ) *n.* 一盤

**A2**: I'd ask the waiter for a new dish. If he didn't bring me one, then I'd speak to the manager.

我會要求服務生給我新的一盤。如果他不給我,那我就會跟經理說。

**A3**: I'd ask the waiter, "Isn't this dish supposed to be hot? I think it's been sitting around too long."

我會問服務生:「這盤菜不是應該是熱的嗎?我想它放太久了。」

~~~~~~~~~~~~~~~~~~

3. **Q**: The window in your classroom is broken. You didn't break it, but your teacher thinks you did. What will you say?

你教室的窗戶破了。你沒有打破窗戶,但是你的老師認為你有。你會說什麼?

【註】 *ask sb. for* 向某人要求　　dish〔dɪʃ〕*n.* 一盤菜
　　　 *speak to sb.* 對某人說
　　　 manager〔'mænɪdʒɚ〕*n.* 經理　　ask〔æsk〕*v.* 問
　　　 suppose〔sə'poz〕*v.* 推測　　*be suppose to V.* 應該~
　　　 hot〔hɑt〕*adj.* 熱的　　sit〔sɪt〕*v.* 擱置
　　　 long〔lɔŋ〕*adv.* 久地;長時間地
　　　 window〔'wɪndo〕*n.* 窗戶
　　　 classroom〔'klæs,rum〕*n.* 教室
　　　 broken〔'brokən〕*adj.* 破裂的
　　　 break〔brek〕*v.* 打破

**A1**：I'll say, "It wasn't me who broke it.　I don't know who is at fault, but I'll help to clean it up."
我會說：「不是我打破的。我不知道那是誰的錯，但是我會幫忙清理乾淨。」

**A2**：I'll say, " No, it wasn't me.　Please don't blame me for something I didn't do."　我會說：「不，不是我打破的。請不要爲了我沒做的事而責備我。」

**A3**：I'll say, "I didn't break it.　If I had, I would admit it.　I wouldn't lie about it."　我會說：「我沒有打破窗戶。如果我有，我會承認。我不會說謊。」

---

**4. Q**：Your car breaks down while you are driving.　You call a mechanic for help.　What will you say?
當你正在開車的時候，你的車故障了。你打電話給機械工人求助。你會說什麼？

【註】　fault ( fɔlt ) *n.* 過錯　　***at fault*** 有過錯；有責任
help ( hɛlp ) *v. n.* 幫忙　　clean ( klin ) *v.* 打掃
***clean up*** 打掃乾淨　　blame ( blem ) *v.* 責怪
***blame sb. for sth.*** 因爲某事責備某人
something ('sʌmθɪŋ ) *pron.* 某事；某物
admit ( əd'mɪt ) *v.* 承認　　lie ( laɪ ) *v.* 說謊
***break down*** 故障　　while ( hwaɪl ) *conj.* 當…的時候
drive ( draɪv ) *v.* 開車　　call ( kɔl ) *v.* 打電話給
***call sb. for help*** 打電話給某人求助
mechanic ( mə'kænɪk ) *n.* 機械工人

**A1**：I'll say, "Hello. I need some help. My car broke down. Could you come out here and take a look?"

我會說：「哈囉。我需要一些幫助。我的車子故障了。你可以來這裡看一看嗎？」

**A2**：I'll say, "Hello. There is something wrong with my car. It broke down while I was driving. Can you come and see what's the matter?"

我會說：「哈囉。我的車子有問題。我正在開車的時候，車子故障了。你可以過來看看怎麼了嗎？」

**A3**：I'll say, "Hello. I need a tow truck. My car is at the corner of Main Street and First Avenue. How long will it take you to get here?"

我會說：「哈囉。我需要一輛拖吊車。我的車子在大街和第一大道的轉角。你們到這裡需要多久？」

【註】 hello〔hə'lo〕*interj.* 哈囉　　***come out*** 出來
***talk a look*** 看一看　　wrong〔rɔŋ〕*adj.* 故障的
***there is something wrong with***～ ～有問題
matter〔'mætɚ〕*n.* 事情；問題
***What's the matter?*** 怎麼了？　　tow〔to〕*n.* 拖
truck〔trʌk〕*n.* 卡車　　***tow truck*** 拖吊車
corner〔'kɔrnɚ〕*n.* 轉角　　main〔men〕*adj.* 主要的
street〔strit〕*n.* 街道　　avenue〔'ævə,nju〕*n.* 大道
***How long will it take***～? ～需要多久？
***get here*** 到這裡

**5. Q** : You are shopping in a department store and you see a shirt that you like. There is no price on the shirt. What will you say to the salesclerk?

你在百貨公司裡購物，然後看到一件你喜歡的襯衫。襯衫上並沒有標價。你會跟店員說什麼？

**A1** : I'll say, "Hi. I really like this shirt. I might want to buy it, but I need to know what the price is first. Could you check for me?"

我會說：「嗨。我真的很喜歡這件襯衫。我可能會想買，但是我想先知道價錢。你可以幫我查一下嗎？」

**A2** : I'll say, "Can you tell me how much this shirt is? I really like it but I won't buy it if it's too expensive."

我會說：「你可以告訴我這件襯衫多少錢嗎？我真的很喜歡，但是如果太貴，我就不會買了。」

**A3** : I'll say, " This is a great shirt. Do you know how much it costs? I'm interested in buying it."

我會說：「這是件很棒的襯衫。你知道它值多少錢嗎？我有興趣想買。」

【註】 shop〔ʃɑp〕v. 購物　　shirt〔ʃɜt〕n. 襯衫
price〔praɪs〕n. 價格
salesclerk〔'selz,klɜk〕n. 店員
hi〔haɪ〕interj. 嗨　　check〔tʃɛk〕v. 查看
great〔gret〕adj. 很棒的　　cost〔kɔst〕v. 值（…錢）
***be interested in*** 對…有興趣

**6. Q** : You have a bad cold.  You don't want to go to work today, so you call your office.  What do you say to the person who answers the phone?

你感了重感冒。你今天不想去上班，所以你打電話到辦公室。你會跟接電話的人說什麼？

**A1** : I would say, "Hi.  This is Sue.  I'm afraid I won't be coming in to work today.  I have a terrible cold. I really need to stay at home and take a rest."

我會說：「嗨。我是蘇。恐怕我今天不會去上班了。我得了重感冒。我真的需要待在家裡休息。」

**A2** : I would say, "Hello.  This is John.  I'm calling in sick today.  Would you please tell the boss for me? Tell him I'm very sorry and I hope I'll see him tomorrow."  我會說：「哈囉。我是約翰。我今天打電話來請病假。可以請你幫我跟老闆說嗎？告訴他我很抱歉，我希望明天可以見到他。」

【註】 bad〔bæd〕adj. 嚴重的　　cold〔kold〕n. 感冒
　　*go to work* 去上班　　office〔'ɔfɪs〕n. 辦公室
　　person〔'pɜsn̩〕n. 人　　answer〔'ænsɚ〕v. 接（電話）
　　phone〔fon〕n. 電話　　afraid〔ə'fred〕adj. 恐怕…的
　　*come in* 進來　　terrible〔'tɛrəbl̩〕adj. 嚴重的
　　stay〔ste〕v. 停留　　rest〔rɛst〕n. 休息
　　*take a rest* 休息一下　　*call in sick* 打電話來請病假
　　boss〔bɔs〕n. 老闆

**A3**：I would say, "Hi. This is Diane. I need to take a sick day. I'm really under the weather and I'm on my way to see the doctor. I'll call in later and let you know what he says." 我會說：「嗨。我是黛安。我需要請病假。我真的很不舒服，我正在去看醫生的途中。我晚一點會再打來，讓你知道醫生說了什麼。」

---

7. **Q** ：You have been invited to dinner at your friend's house. You should arrive at 6:30, but you know you are going to be late, so you call your friend. What will you say? 你被邀請到朋友家吃晚餐。你應該在六點半抵達，但是你知道你就要遲到了，所以你打電話給你的朋友。你會說什麼？

**A1**：I'd say, "Hi. I'm afraid I'm running a little late. I should get there around a quarter to seven. I hope that's OK. See you soon!" 我會說：「嗨。恐怕我會有點遲到。我大概六點四十五分才會到。希望這樣沒關係。待會見！」

【註】 *sick day* 病假　　*take a sick day* 請病假
weather ('wɛðɚ ) *n.* 天氣　　*be under the weather* 不舒服
*on one's way to* ~　在某人去~的途中
later ('letɚ ) *adv.* 之後　　invite ( ɪn'vaɪt ) *v.* 邀請
arrive ( ə'raɪv ) *v.* 到達　　late ( let ) *adj.* 遲到的
*I'm running a little late.* 我會有點遲到。
 ( = *I'm going to be a little late.* )
*get there* 到那裡　　around ( ə'raʊnd ) *adv.* 大約
quarter ('kwɔrtɚ ) *n.* 一刻鐘；十五分鐘
*a quarter to seven* 差十五分鐘七點；六點四十五分
soon ( sun ) *adv.* 馬上；一會兒　　*See you soon!* 待會見！

**A2**: I'd say, "I'm really sorry, but I'm not going to make it by 6:30. Traffic is really terrible. Please go ahead and eat without me. I'll see you when I get there."

我會說:「我真的很抱歉,但是我沒辦法在六點半的時候到。交通狀況真的很糟。請不用等我直接開飯。到時候見。」

**A3**: I'd say, "Hi. I know I should be there at 6:30, but I'm going to be late. I don't want to ruin your dinner, so please start eating without me. I'll get there as soon as I can."

我會說:「嗨。我知道我應該六點半到,但是我會遲到。我不想破壞你們的晚餐,所以請直接開始用餐,不用等我。我會儘快到達。」

【註】 *make it* 能來　　by〔baɪ〕*prep.* 在…之前
traffic〔'træfɪk〕*n.* 交通
terrible〔'tɛrəbl〕*adj.* 糟糕的
*go ahead* 請便;進行　　ruin〔'ruɪn〕*v.* 破壞
start〔stɑrt〕*v.* 開始　　*as soon as one can* 儘快

＊請將下列自我介紹的句子再唸一遍,請開始:

My seat number is (複試座位號碼), and my test number is (初試准考證號碼).

# 初級英語檢定測驗第二階段

# 寫作口説能力測驗②

## 寫作能力測驗

本測驗共有兩部份。第一部份為單句寫作，第二部份為段落寫作。
測驗時間為 40 分鐘。

### 第一部份：單句寫作

請將答案寫在答案紙上對應的題號旁，如有文法、用字、拼字、
標點符號、大小寫等之錯誤，將予扣分。

### 第 1～5 題：句子改寫

請依題目之提示，將原句依指定型式改寫，並將改寫的句子完整
地寫在答案紙上。

注意：須寫出提示之文字及標點符號。

例：題目：I am fine.

　　　　She ＿＿＿＿＿＿＿.

在答案紙上寫：***She is fine.***

1. Peter called John at 9:00 yesterday.

   Who did ＿＿＿＿＿＿＿＿＿＿＿＿＿＿＿＿＿＿＿?

2. Where is the convenience store?

   Do you know ＿＿＿＿＿＿＿＿＿＿＿＿＿＿＿＿＿?

3. Patty plays golf every weekend.

   _____ now.

4. Jason picked some flowers for his girlfriend.

   Jason picked his _____.

5. My sister is studying in Japan.

   _____ since 2005.

第 6～10 題：句子合併

　　請依照題目指示，將兩句合併成一句。並將合併的句子完整地寫在答案紙上。

　　注意：須寫出提示之文字及標點符號。

例：題目：John has a cap.

　　　　　The cap is purple.

　　　　　John _____ cap.

　　在答案紙上寫：***John has a purple cap.***

6. We decided to cancel the trip.

   The tickets were so expensive.

   Since _____.

7. I live in this town.

   The town is famous for its seafood.

   I _____,which _____.

8. George got all of the test questions correct.

   Alice failed the test.

   George _____.

9. Remember to close the window.

   You leave the apartment.

   When _____.

10. We could have caught the train.

    You had run faster.

    We _____ if _____.


第 11～15 題：重組

　　請將題目中所有提示的字詞整合成一有意義的句子，並將重組的
　　句子完整地寫在答案紙上。

　　注意：須寫出提示之文字及標點符號。(答案中必須使用所有提
　　　　　示的字詞，且不能隨意增減字詞，否則不予計分。)

例：題目：John _____.

　　　　　this morning / late / was / again

　　在答案紙上寫：***John was late again this morning.***


11. I _____.

    bring / forgot / to / an umbrella

12. This _____.

the best / in town / pizza and pasta / serves / restaurant

13. Remember to _____.

the book / when / put back / are finished / on the shelf / you

14. I _____.

the meeting / because / the report / postponed / until /
not finished / is / tomorrow

15. Henry told me _____.

in Taichung / to school / that / he / went

## 第二部份：段落寫作

題目：有一天，湯姆（Tom）和瑪莉（Mary）一起去夜行性
動物館（Nocturnal Animal House）參觀。請根據圖
片內容寫一篇約 50 字的簡短描述。

# 口說能力測驗

＊請在 15 秒內完成並唸出下列自我介紹的句子，請開始：

My seat number is （複試座位號碼）, and my test number is （初試准考證號碼）.

## I. 複誦

共五題。題目不印在試題上，由耳機播出，每題播出兩次，兩次之間大約有一到二秒的間隔。聽完兩次後，請馬上複誦一次。

## II. 朗讀句子與短文

共有五個句子及一篇短文，請先利用一分鐘的時間閱讀試題上的句子與短文，然後在一分鐘內以正常的速度，清楚正確的朗讀一遍。

One　: I'm going to the park on Saturday.

Two　: Which would you like, coffee or tea?

Three : Is this the way to Main Street?

Four　: You really did a good job.

Five　: I hung my jacket in the closet.

Six : Next Monday is a holiday. That means we will have a three-day weekend. I plan to visit my aunt and uncle. They live in a small town near a beach. I like to stay with them because I can go swimming every day. Besides that, my aunt is a great cook, and my uncle will take me fishing. I can't wait to go there!

## III. 回答問題

共七題。題目不印在試題上，由耳機播出，每題播出兩次，兩次之間大約有一到二秒的間隔。聽完兩次後，請馬上回答，每題回答時間為 15 秒，請在作答時間內儘量的表達。

* 請將下列自我介紹的句子再唸一遍，請開始：

My seat number is （複試座位號碼）, and my test number is （初試准考證號碼）.

# 寫作口說能力測驗 ② 詳解

## 寫作能力測驗詳解

### 第一部份：單句寫作

第 1～5 題：句子改寫

1. Peter called John at 9:00 yesterday.

   Who did _____?

   重點結構： 肯定句改為疑問句

   解　答： <u>Who did Peter call at 9:00 yesterday?</u>

   句型分析： Who＋did＋主詞＋原形動詞＋時間副詞？

   說　明： 這一題將過去式直述句改為 who 問句，主詞與助動詞須倒裝，故 did 後面放主詞 Peter，而助動詞後面的動詞須用原形，因此 called 須改成 call。

   * call〔kɔl〕v. 打電話給

2. Where is the convenience store?

   Do you know _____?

   重點結構： 直接問句改為間接問句

   解　答： <u>Do you know where the convenience store is?</u>

   句型分析： Do you know＋where＋主詞＋動詞？

說　明：Do you know 後面須接受詞，故直接問句 Where is the convenience store? 須改爲間接問句當受詞，即「疑問詞＋主詞＋動詞」的形式。

＊ convenience〔kən'vinjəns〕n. 方便；便利
***convenience store*** 便利商店

3. Patty plays golf every weekend.

＿＿＿＿＿＿＿＿＿＿＿＿＿＿＿＿＿＿＿＿＿＿＿ now.

重點結構：現在進行式

解　答：<u>Patty is playing golf now.</u>

句型分析：主詞＋be 動詞＋現在分詞＋時間副詞

說　明：時間副詞改爲 now，表示現在正在進行的動作，故動詞時態須改爲「現在進行式」，即「be 動詞＋現在分詞」的形式，主詞 Patty 爲單數，故 bc 動詞用 is。

＊ play〔ple〕v. 打（球）　　golf〔gɑlf〕n. 高爾夫球
weekend〔'wik'ɛnd〕n. 週末

4. Jason picked some flowers for his girlfriend.
Jason picked his ＿＿＿＿＿＿＿＿＿＿＿＿＿＿＿＿＿.

重點結構：pick 做授與動詞的用法

解　答：<u>Jason picked his girlfriend some flowers.</u>

句型分析：主詞＋pick＋直接受詞（人）＋間接受詞（物）

　說　　明：pick（摘）有兩種用法：

$\left\{ \begin{array}{l} ① \ pick + sb. + sth. \\ ② \ pick + sth. + for + sb. \end{array} \right.$

　　　　　　本題的用法為第一種。

* pick〔pɪk〕v. 摘
  girlfriend〔'gɝl,frɛnd〕n. 女朋友

5. My sister is studying in Japan.

　_____ since 2005.

　重點結構：since（自從）的用法

　解　　答：<u>My sister has studied in Japan since 2005.</u>
　　　　　　或 <u>My sister has been studying in Japan since 2005.</u>

　句型分析：主詞 + have/has + 過去分詞 + since 2005
　　　　　　或 主詞 + have/has been + 現在分詞 + since 2005

　說　　明：這題的本意是「我姐姐正在日本唸書」，要改寫成
　　　　　　加了 since（自從…）引導的副詞子句，所以可用
　　　　　　表「從過去持續到現在的動作或狀態」的「現在完
　　　　　　成式」，即「have/has + 過去分詞」，或用表「從過
　　　　　　去某時間開始一直繼續到現在，且仍在進行的動作」
　　　　　　的「現在完成進行式」，即「have/has been + 現在
　　　　　　分詞」。前者強調「時間的經過」，後者強調「動作
　　　　　　的持續」。

* study〔'stʌdɪ〕v. 讀書　　Japan〔dʒə'pæn〕n. 日本

第 6～10 題：句子合併

6. We decided to cancel the trip.

The tickets were so expensive.

Since _____.

> 　重點結構：since（因為、既然）的用法
>
> 　解　答：<u>Since the tickets were so expensive, we decided</u> <u>to cancel the trip.</u>
>
> 　句型分析：Since + 主詞 + be 動詞 + 形容詞 + , + 主詞 + 動詞
>
> 　說　明：這題的意思是「因為車票很貴，所以我們決定取消 旅行」，since 在此為表示原因的從屬連接詞，意思 與 because 相同，但語氣稍弱，常放在句首。
>
> ＊ decide〔dɪˋsaɪd〕v. 決定　　　cancel〔ˋkænsḷ〕v. 取消
>
> 　trip〔trɪp〕n. 旅行　　　ticket〔ˋtɪkɪt〕n. 車票
>
> 　expensive〔ɪkˋspɛnsɪv〕adj. 昂貴的

7. I live in this town.

The town is famous for its seafood.

I _____, which _____.

> 　重點結構：關係代名詞 which 的用法
>
> 　解　答：<u>I live in this town, which is famous for its</u> <u>seafood.</u>
>
> 　句型分析：主詞 + 動詞 + , + which + 形容詞子句

說　明：which 爲關係代名詞，引導形容詞子句，修飾先行
　　　　詞 this town。在這裡要注意的是，which 在此爲
　　　　補述用法，是對先行詞 this town 的補充說明，所
　　　　以 which 和先行詞 this town 之間要有逗點。

* live ( lɪv ) v. 居住　　town ( taʊn ) n. 城鎮
famous ('feməs ) adj. 有名的
**be famous for** 以～而有名　　seafood ('si͵fud ) n. 海鮮


8. George got all of the test questions correct.

Alice failed the test.

George _____.

重點結構：but 的用法

解　答：George got all of the test questions correct,
　　　　but Alice failed the test.

句型分析：主詞 + 動詞 + , + but + 主詞 + 動詞

說　明：依題示，「喬治所有的測驗題都答對」，和「艾莉
　　　　絲測驗不及格」，用反義連接詞 but 來連接前後所
　　　　說意義恰好相反或相互對比的句子，並且用逗點
　　　　來分隔 but 所連接的對等子句。

* get ( gɛt ) v. 獲得；得到　　test ( tɛst ) n. 測驗
question ('kwɛstʃən ) n. 問題
correct ( kə'rɛkt ) adj. 正確的
fail ( fel ) v. ( 考試 ) 不及格

9. Remember to close the window.

   You leave the apartment.

   When _____.

   > 重點結構：when（當…的時候）的用法
   >
   > 解　答：<u>When you leave the apartment, remember to</u>
   > <u>close the window.</u>
   >
   > 句型分析：When + 主詞 + 動詞 + , + remember to V.
   >
   > 説　明：when 在此為連接詞，引導表「時間」的副詞子句，
   > 故先寫 you leave the apartment，再寫主要子句
   > remember to close the window，並且用逗點分
   > 隔二個子句。
   >
   > * remember〔rɪ'mɛmbɚ〕v. 記得
   > close〔kloz〕v. 關　　window〔'wɪndo〕n. 窗戶
   > leave〔liv〕v. 離開　　apartment〔ə'pɑrtmənt〕n. 公寓

10. We could have caught the train.

    You had run faster.

    We _____ if _____.

    > 重點結構：if 的用法
    >
    > 解　答：<u>We could have caught the train if you had run</u>
    > <u>faster.</u>
    >
    > 句型分析：主詞 + should/would/could/might + have +
    > 過去分詞 + if + 主詞 + had + 過去分詞

說　明：if（如果）為連接詞，引導表「條件」的副詞子句。
故 if 後面放 you had run faster，主要子句為 we
could have caught the train，句意為「如果你跑快
一點，我們可能就趕上火車了」，為與過去事實相反
的假設語氣。

* catch〔kætʃ〕v. 趕上　　train〔tren〕n. 火車

第 11～15 題：重組

11. I _____.

bring / forgot / to / an umbrella

重點結構：forget 的用法

解　答：I forgot to bring an umbrella.

句型分析：主詞 + forget + to V.

說　明：forget（忘記）有兩種用法：
① forget + to V.：忘記去做～（動作未做）
② forget + V-ing：忘記做過～（動作已做）
依句意，我忘記帶雨傘，用「forget + to V.」表示。

* bring〔brɪŋ〕v. 攜帶　　umbrella〔ʌmˈbrɛlə〕n. 雨傘

12. This _____.

the best / in town / pizza and pasta / serves / restaurant

重點結構：句子基本結構

解　答：This restaurant serves the best pizza and pasta
in town.

句型分析：主詞＋動詞＋受詞

說　明：這題的意思是說「這家餐廳供應城裡最棒的披薩
和義大利麵」，主詞為 This restaurant，後面接
動詞 serves，the best pizza and pasta in town
為 serves 的受詞，置於句尾。

\* restaurant ('rɛstərənt ) *n.* 餐廳　　serve ( sɜv ) *v.* 供應
best ( bɛst ) *adj.* 最棒的　　pizza ('pitsə ) *n.* 披薩
pasta ('pɑstə ) *n.* 義大利麵　　town ( taun ) *n.* 城鎮

13. Remember to ＿＿＿＿＿＿＿＿＿＿＿＿＿＿＿＿＿＿.

the book / when / put back / are finished / on the shelf / you

重點結構：remember 和 when 的用法

解　答：<u>Remember to put back the book on the shelf
when you are finished.</u>

句型分析：Remember to V. + when + 主詞 + be 動詞 + 形容詞

說　明：remember（記得）有兩種用法：
　　① remember + to V.：記得去做～（動作未做）
　　② remember + V-ing：記得做過～（動作已做）
依句意，「當你用完書後，記得要放回架子上」，用
「remember + to V.」來表示；when 為連接詞，引
導副詞子句 you are finished。

\* shelf ( ʃɛlf ) *n.* 架子
finished ('finiʃt ) *adj.* 用完的；完成的

14. I _____.

the meeting / because / the report / postponed / until /
not finished / is / tomorrow

重點結構：until 和 because 的用法

解　答：I postponed the meeting until tomorrow because
the report is not finished.

句型分析：主詞＋動詞＋until＋時間副詞＋because＋主詞
＋be 動詞＋形容詞

説　明：until（直到…）在句中為介系詞，until tomorrow
修飾主要子句的動詞 postponed，because 引導表
「原因」的副詞子句。本題的意思為，「我把會議
延到明天，因為報告尚未完成」。

\* postpone〔post'pon〕v. 延期　　meeting〔'mitɪŋ〕n. 會議
report〔rɪ'port〕n. 報告　　finish〔'fɪnɪʃ〕v. 完成

15. Henry told me _____.

in Taichung / to school / that / he / went

重點結構：that 引導名詞子句

解　答：Henry told me that he went to school in
Taichung.

句型分析：主詞＋動詞＋that＋主詞＋動詞

説　明：Henry told me 後面須接受詞，由 that 引導的名
詞子句 he went to school in Taichung 當受詞，
句意為「亨利告訴我他在台中上學」。

\* *Taichung* 台中

## 第二部份：段落寫作

【作文範例】

    ***One day*** Tom invited Mary to go to the zoo. They went to the Nocturnal Animal House. Tom took Mary's hand and they walked in. It was dark inside. When he walked outside, Tom looked at the girl holding his hand. The girl was not Mary! Then the strange woman said, "I'm married." Tom was shocked and Mary was angry. Poor Tom.

  * invite ( ɪn'vaɪt ) v. 邀請    zoo ( zu ) n. 動物園
    nocturnal ( nɑk'tɝnḷ ) adj. 夜間活動的
    animal ('ænəmḷ ) n. 動物    house ( haʊs ) n. 房子
    ***Nocturnal Animal House*** 夜行性動物館
    ***took one's hand*** 牽某人的手
    ***walk in*** 走進去    dark ( dɑrk ) adj. 暗的
    inside ('ɪn'saɪd ) adv. 在裡面
    outside ('aʊt'saɪd ) adv. 到外面    ***look at*** 看著
    hold ( hold ) v. 握住    then ( ðɛn ) adv. 然後
    strange ( strendʒ ) adj. 陌生的
    married ('mærɪd ) adv. 已婚的
    shocked ( ʃɑkt ) adj. 震驚的
    angry ('æŋgrɪ ) adj. 生氣的    poor ( pʊr ) adj. 可憐的

# 口說能力測驗詳解

\* 請在15秒內完成並唸出下列自我介紹的句子，請開始：

My seat number is （複試座位號碼）, and my test number is
（初試准考證號碼）.

## I. 複誦

共五題。題目不印在試題上，由耳機播出，每題播出兩次，兩次之間大約有一到二秒的間隔。聽完兩次後，請馬上複誦一次。

1. What a beautiful view! 這個景色真漂亮！

2. Please turn to page four. 請翻到第四頁。

3. Is this your bag? 這是你的包包嗎？

4. I enjoy singing. 我喜歡唱歌。

5. Your dog is so cute. 你的狗真可愛。

【註】 view〔vju〕n. 景色　　turn〔tɜn〕v. 翻（頁）
　　　page〔pedʒ〕n. 頁　　bag〔bæg〕n. 袋子；包包
　　　enjoy〔ɪn'dʒɔɪ〕v. 喜歡　　sing〔sɪŋ〕v. 唱歌
　　　cute〔kjut〕adj. 可愛的

## II. 朗讀句子與短文

共有五個句子及一篇短文，請先利用一分鐘的時間閱讀試題上的句子與短文，然後在一分鐘內以正常的速度，清楚正確的朗讀一遍。

One　: I'm going to the park on Saturday.
　　　我禮拜六將要去公園。

Two　: Which would you like, coffee or tea?
　　　你想要哪一個，咖啡還是茶？

Three : Is this the way to Main Street?
　　　這是去大街的路嗎？

Four　: You really did a good job.
　　　你真的做得很好。

Five　: I hung my jacket in the closet.
　　　我把我的外套掛在衣櫥裡。

【註】 park ( park ) n. 公園
　　　Saturday ('sætə‚de ) n. 星期六
　　　which ( hwɪtʃ ) pron. 哪一個　　like ( laɪk ) v. 喜歡
　　　coffee ('kɔfɪ ) n. 咖啡　　tea ( ti ) n. 茶
　　　way ( we ) n. 路　　main ( men ) adj. 主要的
　　　street ( strit ) n. 街道　　really ('riəlɪ ) adv. 真地
　　　job ( dʒɑb ) n. 任務；工作　　*do a good job* 做得很好
　　　hang ( hæŋ ) v. 掛　　jacket ('dʒækɪt ) n. 外套
　　　closet ('klɑzɪt ) n. 衣櫥

Six ： Next Monday is a holiday. That means we will have a three-day weekend. I plan to visit my aunt and uncle. They live in a small town near a beach. I like to stay with them because I can go swimming every day. Besides that, my aunt is a great cook, and my uncle will take me fishing. I can't wait to go there!

下個星期一是假日。那就表示我們將會有三天的週末假期。我計畫去拜訪我的阿姨和姨丈。他們住在靠近海邊的一個小鎮。我喜歡到他們家作客，因為我可以每天去游泳。除此之外，我阿姨很會做菜，而且我的姨丈會帶我去釣魚。我等不及要去那裡了！

【註】 next 〔nɛkst〕 adj. 下一個的
　　　 Monday 〔'mʌnde〕 n. 星期一
　　　 holiday 〔'halə,de〕 n. 假日　　 mean 〔min〕 v. 意思是
　　　 weekend 〔'wik'ɛnd〕 n. 週末　　 plan 〔plæn〕 v. 計畫
　　　 visit 〔'vɪzɪt〕 v. 拜訪　　 aunt 〔ænt〕 n. 阿姨
　　　 uncle 〔'ʌŋkl̩〕 n. 姨丈　　 live 〔lɪv〕 v. 住
　　　 small 〔smɔl〕 adj. 小的　　　 town 〔taʊn〕 n. 城鎮
　　　 near 〔nɪr〕 prep. 在…的附近　　 beach 〔bitʃ〕 n. 海邊
　　　 stay 〔ste〕 v. ( 在別人家 ) 作客 < with >
　　　 swim 〔swɪm〕 v. 游泳　　 *go swimming* 去游泳
　　　 besides 〔bɪ'saɪdz〕 prep. 除了…之外
　　　 great 〔gret〕 adj. 很棒的　　 cook 〔kʊk〕 n. 廚師
　　　 fishing 〔'fɪʃɪŋ〕 n. 釣魚　　 wait 〔wet〕 v. 等
　　　 *I can't wait to～* 我等不及要～　　 *go there* 去那裡

## III. 回答問題

共七題。題目不印在試題上，由耳機播出，每題播出兩次，兩次之間大約有一到二秒的間隔。聽完兩次後，請馬上回答，每題回答時間為 15 秒，請在作答時間內儘量的表達。

**1. Q** : You buy something in a shop. When you receive your change, it is not enough. What do you say to the clerk? 你在商店裡買東西。當你收到找給你的錢時，錢不夠。你會跟店員說什麼？

**A1** : I'd say, "Excuse me, but I think you made a mistake. You gave me the incorrect change. Would you please check again?"
我會說：「不好意思，但我想你弄錯了。你找給我的錢不正確。可以請你再檢查一次嗎？」

**A2** : I'd say, "Sorry, but I don't think this is right. You've shortchanged me." 我會說：「抱歉，但我不認為這個是金額是正確的。你少找錢給我。」

【註】 receive〔rɪ'siv〕v. 收到
change〔tʃendʒ〕n. 找回的錢；零錢
enough〔ə'nʌf〕adj. 足夠的
clerk〔klɜk〕n. 店員　　mistake〔mə'stek〕n. 錯誤
incorrect〔ˌɪnkə'rɛkt〕adj. 不正確的
check〔tʃɛk〕v. 檢查　　again〔ə'gɛn〕adv. 再一次
right〔raɪt〕adj. 正確的
shortchange〔ˌʃɔrt'tʃendʒ〕v. 少找錢給…

**A3**: I'd say, "Wait a minute. This is not enough change. Would you please check the total again?"
我會說：「等一下。你找的錢不夠。可以請你再檢查一次總額嗎？」

2. **Q**: You want to take the bus. The bus costs 20 dollars but you have only a one-hundred note. Ask a bystander to help you.
你想搭公車。搭公車需要二十元，但你身上只有一張一百元紙鈔。請一位旁邊的人幫你。

**A1**: "Excuse me. Do you have change for a hundred? I'd really appreciate it." 「不好意思。你有一百元的零錢嗎？我會非常感激你的。」

**A2**: "Hello. Can you help me out? I want to take the bus, but I don't have any change. Can you change this hundred for me?"
「哈囉。你可以幫我嗎？我想搭公車，但我身上沒有任何零錢。你可以幫我把這一百元換成零錢嗎？」

【註】 minute ('mɪnɪt ) n. 分鐘　　***wait a minute*** 等一下
total ('totl̩ ) n. 總額　　take ( tek ) v. 搭乘
cost ( kɔst ) v. 需要…錢　　dollar ('dɑlə ) n. 元
hundred ('hʌndrəd ) n. 百　　note ( not ) n. 紙鈔
ask ( æsk ) v. 請求　　bystander ('baɪ,stændə ) n. 旁觀者
appreciate ( ə'priʃɪ,et ) v. 感激　　***help sb. out*** 幫助某人
change ( tʃendʒ ) v. (為某人) 把 (鈔票等) 換成零錢 <*for*>

**A3**："Hi. Sorry to bother you, but I need to get some change for the bus. Could you break a hundred by any chance?" 「嗨。抱歉打擾你，但我需要一些零錢搭公車。你碰巧可以把一百元找開嗎？」

---

**3. Q**：You call your doctor's office to make an appointment for a checkup. What do you say to the receptionist? 你打電話到醫生的診所預約健康檢查。你會對櫃檯人員說什麼？

**A1**：I'd say, "I'd like to see the doctor. Can I make an appointment? Is next Thursday possible?" 我會說：「我想要看醫生。我可以預約嗎？下個星期四有可能嗎？」

**A2**：I'd say, "Hello, I need to make an appointment. It's for a checkup. Can you tell me when the doctor is free?" 我會說：「哈囉，我要預約。我想要做健康檢查。你可以告訴我醫生什麼時候有空嗎？」

【註】 bother〔'baðɚ〕v. 打擾
break〔brek〕v. 將（大鈔）換零
chance〔tʃæns〕n. 機會；運氣　　*by any chance* 碰巧
office〔'ɔfɪs〕n. 診所
appointment〔ə'pɔɪntmənt〕n. 預約
checkup〔'tʃɛkˌʌp〕n. 健康檢查
receptionist〔rɪ'sɛpʃənɪst〕n. 櫃檯人員
Thursday〔'θɝzde〕n. 星期四
possible〔'pɑsəbl̩〕adj. 可能的　　free〔fri〕adj. 有空的

**A3**：I'd say, "I'd like to make an appointment with the doctor. It's not an emergency, just a checkup. Any weekday afternoon would be fine."

我會說：「我想和醫生預約。沒有很緊急，只是做健康檢查而已。任何一天平常日的下午都可以。」

---

**4. Q** ：Imagine you locked yourself out of your house. What would you do?

想像一下你把自己鎖在家門外。你會怎麼做？

**A1**：I'd call my brother. He has an extra key to my house. I'd ask him to come over as soon as possible.

我會打電話給我哥哥。他有我家裡的備份鑰匙。我會要他儘快過來。

【註】　emergency ( ɪ'mɝdʒənsɪ ) *n.* 緊急情況
　　　　weekday ('wik,de ) *n.* 平日
　　　　fine ( faɪn ) *adj.* 很好的
　　　　imagine ( ɪ'mædʒɪn ) *v.* 想像
　　　　lock ( lɑk ) *v.* 鎖　　*lock sb. out* 把某人鎖在外面
　　　　extra ('ɛkstrə ) *adj.* 額外的
　　　　key ( ki ) *n.* 鑰匙　　*come over* 過來
　　　　*as soon as possible* 儘快

**A2**: I'm afraid I'd have to call a locksmith. I'd use my cell phone. If I didn't have it, I'd ask my neighbor for help. 恐怕我必須找鎖匠來了。我會用我的手機。如果我沒有手機，那我會找鄰居幫忙。

**A3**: I would call a locksmith. Then I'd go to my neighbor's house. I would wait there. If he wasn't at home, I would go to a café or fast-food restaurant. 我會打電話給鎖匠。然後我會去我鄰居家。我會在他家等。如果他不在家，我會去咖啡廳或是速食店。

---

**5. Q** : You are standing in line to buy movie tickets. What do you say to the person selling them? 你正在排隊買電影票。你會對賣票的人說什麼？

**A1**: I'd say, "Hi. I'd like two tickets to the Indiana Jones movie. We want to go to the 7:30 show." 我會說：「嗨。我想買兩張印第安那瓊斯的電影票。我們想要看七點半的那一場。」

**【註】** *I'm afraid~* 恐怕~　　call〔kɔl〕*v.* 叫
locksmith〔'lɑk,smɪθ〕*n.* 鎖匠　　***cell phone*** 手機
neighbor〔'nebɚ〕*n.* 鄰居　　café〔kə'fe〕*n.* 咖啡店
fast-food〔'fæst,fud〕*adj.* 速食的
restaurant〔'rɛstərənt〕*n.* 餐廳
line〔laɪn〕*n.* 行列　　***stand in line*** 排隊
movie〔'muvɪ〕*n.* 電影　　ticket〔'tɪkɪt〕*n.* 票
person〔'pɝsn̩〕*n.* 人　　sell〔sɛl〕*v.* 賣
***Indiana Jones*** 印第安那瓊斯　　show〔ʃo〕*n.* 電影
***go to the 7:30 show*** 去看七點半的電影

**A2**：I'd say, "Are there any seats left for the 8:00 show? I need three adult tickets.　Thanks a lot."

我會說：「八點那一場電影還有剩下任何座位嗎？我需要三張成人票。多謝。」

**A3**：I'd say, "Two adults for the next showing of *Aliens Attack*.　We'd like to sit somewhere in the middle of the theater."

我會說：「兩張成人票，看下一場的「外星人攻擊」。我們想要坐在電影院中間的位置。」

---

**6. Q**　：Imagine that you are taking a walk in the park and it starts to rain heavily.　What would you do in that situation?

想像一下你正在公園裡散步，卻開始下起了傾盆大雨。在那樣的情況下你會怎麼做？

【註】　seat ( sit ) *n.* 座位　　left ( lɛft ) *adj.* 剩下的
adult ( ə'dʌlt ) *n.* 成人　　showing ('ʃoɪŋ ) *n.* 放映；播映
alien ('elɪən , 'eljən ) *n.* 外星人　　attack ( ə'tæk ) *n.* 攻擊
somewhere ('sʌm,hwɛr ) *adv.* 某處
middle ('mɪdl̩ ) *n.* 中間　　*in the middle of* 在…的中間
theater ('θiətɚ ) *n.* 電影院　　*take a walk* 散步
start ( stɑrt ) *v.* 開始　　rain ( ren ) *v.* 下雨
heavily ('hɛvɪlɪ ) *adv.* 猛烈地
situation (,sɪtʃu'eʃən ) *n.* 情況

**A1**: I think I would run. I would just run as fast as I could until I reached some kind of shelter.

我想我會跑。我會盡可能地快跑，一直跑到某個可以避雨的地方。

**A2**: I would just open my umbrella. I always carry an umbrella, so I am always prepared when it starts to rain. But I would still leave the park because it's not pleasant to walk in a heavy rain.

我會打開我的傘。我總是帶著傘，所以開始下雨的時候我總是會有所準備。但是我還是會離開公園，因為在大雨中散步一點都不愉快。

**A3**: I would try to find someplace that I could stay dry. Maybe I would stand under a tree or go to the public restroom in the park. Then I would wait until the rain let up a little before leaving the park. 我會試著找一個不會淋到雨的地方。也許我會站在樹下，或是到公園的公共廁所。然後我會一直等到大雨逐漸停止，才離開公園。

---

**7. Q**: When you go home you want to watch a special program on TV. But you find your sister is already watching something. What do you say to her?

當你回家的時候，你想看電視上一個特別的節目。但是你發現你的姊姊已經在看其他節目了。你會對她說什麼？

【註】 ***as…as one can*** 儘可能…

until〔ən'tɪl〕*conj.* 直到…

reach〔ritʃ〕*v.* 到達

some〔sʌm〕*adj.* 某個

kind〔kaɪnd〕*n.* 種類

***some kind of*** 某種

shelter〔'ʃɛltɚ〕*n.* 避雨的場所

umbrella〔ʌm'brɛlə〕*n.* 雨傘

always〔'ɔlwez〕*adv.* 總是

prepared〔prɪ'pɛrd〕*adj.* 有準備的

pleasant〔'plɛznt〕*adj.* 令人愉快的

heavy〔'hɛvɪ〕*adj.* 猛烈的

***heavy rain*** 大雨

try〔traɪ〕*v.* 嘗試

find〔faɪnd〕*v.* 找到

someplace〔'sʌmples〕*n.* 某處

***stay dry*** 保持乾燥

public〔'pʌblɪk〕*adj.* 公共的

restroom〔'rɛst,rum〕*n.* 廁所（= *rest room*）

***let up*** （雨）逐漸停止

watch〔watʃ〕*v.* 看

special〔'spɛʃəl〕*adj.* 特別的

program〔'progræm〕*n.* 節目

already〔ɔl'rɛdɪ〕*adv.* 已經

**A1**： I will say, "There's a really great program on channel 2.  I think you'd like it.  Would you mind changing the channel?"　我會說：「第二台有一個眞的很好看的節目。我覺得妳會喜歡。妳介不介意轉台？」

**A2**： I will say, "I'd really like to watch another show. It's on only today.  Will you let me watch it?" 我會說：「我眞的很想看另一個節目。只有今天才有播。 妳可以讓我看嗎？」

**A3**： I will say, "Are you really interested in that show? There's something else on that I would like to watch.  Maybe we could watch it together." 我會說：「妳眞的對這個節目有興趣嗎？有播出別的我很 想看的節目。也許我們可以一起看。」

【註】　great〔gret〕*adj.* 很棒的　　channel〔'tʃænl〕*n.* 頻道
mind〔maɪnd〕*v.* 介意　　change〔tʃendʒ〕*v.* 改變
another〔ə'nʌðɚ〕*adj.* 另一的　　show〔ʃo〕*n.* 節目
on〔ɑn〕*adv.* 正在放映的　　let〔lɛt〕*v.* 讓
***be interested in***　對…有興趣　　else〔ɛls〕*adj.* 其他的
***would like to V.***　想要…　　maybe〔'mebi〕*adv.* 或許
together〔tə'gɛðɚ〕*adv.* 一起

＊請將下列自我介紹的句子再唸一遍，請開始：

My seat number is（複試座位號碼）, and my test number is （初試准考證號碼）.

## 初級英語檢定測驗第二階段

# 寫作口說能力測驗③

## 寫作能力測驗

　　本測驗共有兩部份。第一部份為單句寫作，第二部份為段落寫作。測驗時間為 40 分鐘。

### 第一部份：單句寫作

　　請將答案寫在答案紙上對應的題號旁，如有文法、用字、拼字、標點符號、大小寫等之錯誤，將予扣分。

第 1～5 題：句子改寫

　　請依題目之提示，將原句依指定型式改寫，並將改寫的句子<u>完整</u>地寫在答案紙上。

　　注意：須寫出提示之文字及標點符號。

例：題目：I am fine.

　　　　　She _____.

　　在答案紙上寫：***She is fine.***

1. Jane has been waiting for two hours.

   How long _____?

2. David put the letter under the newspaper.

   David _____ on top of _____.

3. The parade will start at three o'clock.

The parade _____ every year.

4. You brought the birthday cake, didn't you?

Did you _____?

5. If he had run to school, he would not have been late.

If he runs _____.

第 6～10 題：句子合併

請依照題目指示，將兩句合併成一句。並將合併的句子完整地寫在答案紙上。

注意：須寫出提示之文字及標點符號。

例：題目：John has a cap.

The cap is purple.

John _____ cap.

在答案紙上寫：***John has a purple cap.***

6. Joan wants to buy the jacket.

The jacket is on sale.

Joan _____ that _____.

7. We shouldn't eat too many sweets.

They are bad for our teeth.

_____, for _____.

8. The amusement park is not open.

   It will not open until 10:00.

   The amusement park will _____ until _____.

9. Elizabeth cooked a delicious meal.

   She cooked the meal for us.

   Elizabeth _____ us _____.

10. Martha takes a taxi to work.

    Martha takes a taxi when it rains.

    Martha takes _____ whenever _____.

第 11～15 題：重組

　　請將題目中所有提示的字詞整合成一有意義的句子，並將重組的
　　句子完整地寫在答案紙上。

　　注意：須寫出提示之文字及標點符號。(答案中必須使用所有提
　　　　　示的字詞，且不能隨意增減字詞，否則不予計分。)

例：題目：John _____.

　　　　　this morning / late / was / again

　　在答案紙上寫：***John was late again this morning.***

11. My classmates _____.

    the race / me / congratulated / winning / on

12. This café _____.

so / somewhere else / open / doesn't / let's go / until / , / nine

13. My sister _____.

to take out / me / told / the trash

14. Should _____.

we / to school / the typhoon / will not / arrive / go / tomorrow / ,

15. How _____?

cake / make / did / delicious / you / this

### 第二部份：段落寫作

題目：有一天，鮑伯（Bob）和克拉克（Clark）一起進入一
間充滿瓦斯味的房間。請根據圖片內容寫一篇約50字
的簡短描述。

# 口說能力測驗

\* 請在 15 秒內完成並唸出下列自我介紹的句子，請開始：

My seat number is <u>（複試座位號碼）</u>, and my test number is <u>（初試准考證號碼）</u>.

## I. 複誦

共五題。題目不印在試題上，由耳機播出，每題播出兩次，兩次之間大約有一到二秒的間隔。聽完兩次後，請馬上複誦一次。

## II. 朗讀句子與短文

共有五個句子及一篇短文，請先利用一分鐘的時間閱讀試題上的句子與短文，然後在一分鐘內以正常的速度，清楚正確的朗讀一遍。

One　：Both Jack and Mary are students.

Two　：The CD is on the table in the living room.

Three：I had a great time at the party.

Four　：You can drive a car, can't you?

Five　：This is not the only way to get here.

Six : Yesterday my friend Linda taught me how to make a cake. First, she took me to the supermarket and we bought all of the ingredients. Then we went back to her house and made the cake. It wasn't hard at all! And it was really delicious. The only bad thing was that we had to wash a lot of dishes and clean the kitchen. It was a mess!

## Ⅲ. 回答問題

共七題。題目不印在試題上，由耳機播出，每題播出兩次，兩次之間大約有一到二秒的間隔。聽完兩次後，請馬上回答，每題回答時間為 15 秒，請在作答時間內儘量的表達。

\* 請將下列自我介紹的句子再唸一遍，請開始：

My seat number is （複試座位號碼）, and my test number is （初試准考證號碼）.

# 寫作口說能力測驗 ③ 詳解

## 寫作能力測驗詳解

### 第一部份：單句寫作

#### 第 1~5 題：句子改寫

1. Jane has been waiting for two hours.

   How long _____?

   > **重點結構：** 肯定句改爲疑問句
   >
   > **解　答：** How long has Jane been waiting?
   >
   > **句型分析：** How long＋have/has＋主詞＋been＋現在分詞？
   >
   > **說　明：** 這一題將現在完成進行式的直述句改爲 How long 的疑問句，助動詞 has 與主詞 Jane 須倒裝，並將句號改成問號，形成問句。
   >
   > \* **wait for** 等待

2. David put the letter under the newspaper.

   David _____ on top of _____.

   > **重點結構：** on top of 的用法
   >
   > **解　答：** David put the newspaper on top of the letter.
   >
   > **句型分析：** 主詞＋動詞＋on top of＋受詞

　　說　明：原意為「信在報紙的下面」，換句話說，「報紙在信
　　　　　　的上面」，故 under 改成 on top of 時，letter 和
　　　　　　newspaper 的位置須互換。

* letter〔'lɛtɚ〕n. 信　　under〔'ʌndɚ〕prep. 在…之下
  newspaper〔'njuz,pepɚ〕n. 報紙　***on top of*** 在…之上

3. The parade will start at three o'clock.

   The parade ＿＿＿＿＿＿＿＿＿＿＿＿＿＿＿＿＿ every year.

   重點結構：現在簡單式的用法

   　解　答：The parade starts at three o'clock every year.

   句型分析：主詞＋動詞（現在簡單式）＋時間副詞

   　說　明：從時間副詞 every year（每年）可知，遊行三點開
   　　　　　　始為一種習慣動作，故動詞時態用「現在簡單式」，
   　　　　　　又 The parade 是第三人稱單數，故動詞 start 須加 s。

   * parade〔pə'red〕n. 遊行　　start〔stɑrt〕v. 開始

4. You brought the birthday cake, didn't you?

   Did you ＿＿＿＿＿＿＿＿＿＿＿＿＿＿＿＿＿？

   重點結構：問句基本結構

   　解　答：Did you bring the birthday cake?

   句型分析：Did＋主詞＋原形動詞？

   　說　明：以助動詞為首的疑問句，須用原形動詞，故 brought
   　　　　　　改為原形 bring。

   * bring〔brɪŋ〕v. 帶來　　birthday〔'bɝθ,de〕n. 生日
     cake〔kek〕n. 蛋糕

5. If he had run to school, he would not have been late.

   If he runs ＿＿＿＿＿＿＿＿＿＿＿＿＿＿＿＿＿＿.

    **重點結構：** 直說法條件句

      **解　答：** <u>If he runs to school, he will not be late.</u>

    **句型分析：** If ＋ 主詞 ＋ 動詞（現在式）＋, ＋ 主詞 ＋
            助動詞否定（未來式）＋ be 動詞 ＋ 形容詞

      **說　明：** 本句句意原為「假如他用跑的去學校，他就不會遲
            到了」，為「與過去事實相反」的假設語氣，由句首
            改成 If he runs 可知，本句要改成直說法，條件句
            「如果他用跑的去學校」，事實上不可能在說現在，
            可見在說未來，但是表「條件」的副詞子句中，不
            能用未來式，要用現在代替未來，而主要子句則不
            受此限制，故可用未來式 he will not be late。

    * run〔rʌn〕v. 跑　　late〔let〕adj. 遲到的

第 6～10 題：句子合併

6. Joan wants to buy the jacket.

   The jacket is on sale.

   Joan ＿＿＿＿＿＿＿ that ＿＿＿＿＿＿＿＿＿＿.

    **重點結構：** that 引導形容詞子句的用法

      **解　答：** <u>Joan wants to buy the jacket that is on sale.</u>

    **句型分析：** 主詞 ＋ 動詞 ＋ 不定詞 ＋ that ＋ 形容詞子句

      **說　明：** that 在此為關係代名詞，代替先行詞 the jacket，
            引導形容詞子句。句意是「瓊想買正在拍賣的那件
            夾克」，故主要子句 Joan wants to buy the jacket
            放在 that 之前，形容詞子句 is on sale 放在 that 之後。

    * jacket〔ˈdʒækɪt〕n. 夾克；外套　　***on sale*** 拍賣

7. We shouldn't eat too many sweets.
   They are bad for our teeth.
   _____, for _____.

    重點結構：for 的用法

    解　答：<u>We shouldn't eat too many sweets, for they are</u>
             <u>bad for our teeth.</u>

    句型分析：主詞＋助動詞＋動詞＋受詞＋, ＋for＋主詞＋
             be 動詞＋形容詞片語

    說　明：for 在此為表示「因為；由於」的對等連接詞，後
             面應接原因，故結果 We shouldn't eat too many
             sweets 放在 for 之前，原因 they are bad for our
             teeth 放在 for 之後。

    \* sweets〔swits〕*n. pl.* 甜食　　teeth〔tiθ〕*n. pl.* 牙齒

8. The amusement park is not open.
   It will not open until 10:00.
   The amusement park will _____ until _____.

    重點結構：「not…until~」的用法

    解　答：<u>The amusement park will not open until 10:00.</u>

    句型分析：主詞＋助動詞＋not＋原形動詞＋until＋時間副詞

    說　明：這題的意思是「遊樂園直到十點才會開始營業」，
             until（直到）為介系詞，後接 10:00 為受詞，當主
             要子句為否定時，句意就會成為「直到~才…」，故
             主詞後面接動詞否定 will not open 後，再接 until
             引導的子句。

    \* amusement〔ə'mjuzmənt〕*n.* 娛樂
      ***amusement park*** 遊樂園　　open〔'opən〕*v.* 開始營業

9. Elizabeth cooked a delicious meal.

She cooked the meal for us.

Elizabeth ＿＿＿＿＿＿＿＿＿ us ＿＿＿＿＿＿＿＿＿＿＿＿＿.

　　重點結構：cook 做授與動詞的用法

　　　解　答：Elizabeth cooked us a delicious meal.

　　句型分析：主詞＋cook＋直接受詞（人）＋間接受詞（物）

　　　說　明：cook（煮；烹調）有兩種用法：
　　　　　　　① cook + *sb.* + *sth.*
　　　　　　　② cook + *sth.* + for + *sb.*
　　　　　　　本題的用法為第一種。

　　* delicious〔dɪ'lɪʃəs〕*adj.* 美味的　　meal〔mil〕*n.* 一餐

10. Martha takes a taxi to work.

Martha takes a taxi when it rains.

Martha takes ＿＿＿＿＿＿＿ whenever ＿＿＿＿＿＿＿＿＿.

　　重點結構：whenever 的用法

　　　解　答：Martha takes a taxi to work whenever it rains.

　　句型分析：主詞＋動詞＋whenever＋主詞＋動詞

　　　說　明：whenever（不論何時）為引導表「時間」的從屬連
　　　　　　　接詞，本句的意思為「只要是下雨的時候，瑪莎就
　　　　　　　坐計程車去上班」。it 在此指「天氣」。

　　* take〔tek〕*v.* 搭乘（交通工具）
　　　taxi〔'tæksɪ〕*n.* 計程車
　　　work〔wɝk〕*v.* 工作　　rain〔ren〕*v.* 下雨

第 11～15 題：重組

11. My classmates ＿＿＿＿＿＿＿＿＿＿＿＿＿＿＿＿＿＿＿＿.

　　the race / me / congratulated / winning / on

　　　　重點結構：congratulate 的用法

　　　　解　答：<u>My classmates congratulated me on winning the race.</u>

　　　　句型分析：主詞 + congratulate + 受詞（人）+ on + 受詞（事）

　　　　說　明：這題的意思是「我的同學恭喜我贏得比賽」。
　　　　　　　　　congratulate 的用法為：「congratulate + *sb.* + on + *sth.*」。

　　　　* classmate〔'klæs,met〕*n.* 同班同學
　　　　　congratulate〔kən'grætʃə,let〕*v.* 恭喜；祝賀
　　　　　win〔wɪn〕*v.* 贏得　　race〔res〕*n.* 競賽；賽跑

12. This café ＿＿＿＿＿＿＿＿＿＿＿＿＿＿＿＿＿＿＿＿.

　　so / somewhere else / open / doesn't / let's go / until / , / nine

　　　　重點結構：so 的用法

　　　　解　答：<u>This café doesn't open until nine, so let's go somewhere else.</u>

　　　　句型分析：主詞 + 動詞否定 + until + 時間副詞 + , + so + 主詞 + 動詞

　　　　說　明：連接詞 so 的用法為：「原因 + , so + 結果」，按照句意，「這間咖啡店九點才會開始營業，所以我們去其

他地方吧」，故先寫原因 This café doesn't open
until nine，再寫結果 so let's go somewhere else。

*　café〔kəˈfe〕n. 咖啡店　　**not…until~**　直到~才…
somewhere〔ˈsʌm͵hwɛr〕adv. 某處　　else〔ɛls〕adv. 其他

13. My sister _____.

to take out / me / told / the trash

　　重點結構：tell 的用法

　　解　答：My sister told me to take out the trash.

　　句型分析：主詞＋tell＋受詞＋to V.

　　說　明：tell 的用法為：「tell *sb.* to V.」表示「告訴某人
　　　　　　去做~」。

*　**take out** 把…拿出去　　trash〔træʃ〕n. 垃圾

14. Should _____.

we / to school / the typhoon / will not / arrive / go / tomorrow / ,

　　重點結構：假設語氣 should 的用法

　　解　答：Should the typhoon arrive tomorrow, we will
　　　　　　not go to school.

　　句型分析：should＋主詞＋動詞＋,＋主詞＋否定助動詞（未
　　　　　　來式）＋動詞

　　說　明：should 表示可能性很小的假設，放在句首，表「萬
　　　　　　一」的意思，後面接引導表「條件」的副詞子句。
　　　　　　本句的意思為「萬一明天颱風來的話，我們就不用
　　　　　　去上學了」。

*　typhoon〔taɪˈfun〕n. 颱風　　arrive〔əˈraɪv〕v. 到達

15. How _____?

cake / make / did / delicious / you / this

　　重點結構： 問句基本結構

　　　解　答： <u>How did you make this delicious cake?</u>

　　句型分析： How + did + 主詞 + 動詞 + 受詞？

　　　説　明： 這一題考問句的基本結構，主詞與助動詞須倒裝，故
　　　　　　　先找出助動詞 did，再找出主詞 you，後面接原形動
　　　　　　　詞 make，this delicious cake 為受詞，放在句尾。

## 第二部份：段落寫作

【作文範例】

　　Bob and Clark are classmates and roommates. ***One day***, they went home after class. Bob opened the door. He could smell gas. They had forgotten to turn off the gas after cooking their breakfast. Just then, Clark lit a cigarette. There was a big explosion and both boys were hurt. Now they are roommates in a hospital.

* classmate ('klæs,met ) *n.* 同班同學
　roommate ('rum,met ) *n.* 室友　　***one day*** 有一天
　class ( klæs ) *n.* 上課　　***after class*** 放學
　smell ( smɛl ) *v.* 聞到　　gas ( gæs ) *n.* 瓦斯
　***turn off*** 關掉　　breakfast ('brɛkfəst ) *n.* 早餐
　***just then*** 就在那時候　　light ( laɪt ) *v.* 點燃
　cigarette ('sɪgə,rɛt ) *n.* 香煙　　explosion ( ɪk'sploʒən ) *n.* 爆炸
　hurt ( hɜt ) *v.* 使受傷【三態同形】　　***be hurt*** 受傷
　hospital ('hɑspɪtl̩ ) *n.* 醫院

# 口說能力測驗詳解

＊請在15秒內完成並唸出下列自我介紹的句子，請開始：

My seat number is （複試座位號碼），and my test number is （初試准考證號碼）.

## I. 複誦

　　共五題。題目不印在試題上，由耳機播出，每題播出兩次，兩次之間大約有一到二秒的間隔。聽完兩次後，請馬上複誦一次。

　　1. I bought a new camera. 我買了一台新相機。

　　2. What time will you come? 你幾點會來？

　　3. I have a headache. 我頭痛。

　　4. He is my best friend. 他是我最好的朋友。

　　5. The game starts at two o'clock. 比賽兩點開始。

【註】　camera〔ˈkæmərə〕 n. 相機
　　　　headache〔ˈhɛdˌek〕 n. 頭痛
　　　　game〔gem〕 n. 比賽
　　　　start〔stɑrt〕 v. 開始
　　　　o'clock〔əˈklɑk〕 adv. …點鐘

## II. 朗讀句子與短文

共有五個句子及一篇短文,請先利用一分鐘的時間閱讀試題上的句子與短文,然後在一分鐘內以正常的速度,清楚正確的朗讀一遍。

One : Both Jack and Mary are students.
傑克和瑪莉兩個都是學生。

Two : The CD is on the table in the living room.
CD 在客廳的桌上。

Three : I had a great time at the party.
我在宴會裡玩得很愉快。

Four : You can drive a car, can't you?
你會開車,不是嗎?

Five : This is not the only way to get here.
這不是來這裡唯一的路。

【註】 *both A and B* A 和 B 兩者　　 Jack〔dʒæk〕*n.* 傑克
*CD* *n.* 雷射唱片 ( = *compact disk* )
*living room* 客廳　　 great〔gret〕*adj.* 很棒的
*have a great time* 玩得很愉快
party〔'partɪ〕*n.* 宴會　　 drive〔draɪv〕*v.* 開(車)
only〔'onlɪ〕*adj.* 唯一的　　 way〔we〕*n.* 道路
*get here* 來這裡

Six ： Yesterday my friend Linda taught me how to make a cake. First, she took me to the supermarket and we bought all of the ingredients. Then we went back to her house and made the cake. It wasn't hard at all! And it was really delicious. The only bad thing was that we had to wash a lot of dishes and clean the kitchen. It was a mess!

昨天我的朋友琳達教我怎麼做蛋糕。首先，她帶我到超級市場，我們買了所有的材料。然後我們回到她家去做蛋糕。那一點都不難！而且蛋糕真的非常的美味。唯一遺憾的是，我們必須洗很多的盤子和打掃廚房。那真是一團亂！

【註】　Linda ('lɪndə ) n. 琳達　　teach ( titʃ ) v. 教
cake ( kek ) n. 蛋糕　　first ( fɜst ) adv. 首先
supermarket ('supɚ,markɪt ) n. 超級市場
ingredient ( ɪn'gridɪənt ) n. 原料；材料
go back 回去　　hard ( hard ) adj. 困難的
not…at all 一點也不…　　really ('riəlɪ ) adv. 真地
delicious ( dɪ'lɪʃəs ) adj. 好吃的
bad ( bæd ) adj. 遺憾的　　wash ( waʃ ) v. 洗
a lot of 很多　　dish ( dɪʃ ) n. 盤子
clean ( klin ) v. 打掃　　kitchen ('kɪtʃɪn ) n. 廚房
mess ( mɛs ) n. 混亂

## Ⅲ. 回答問題

共七題。題目不印在試題上，由耳機播出，每題播出兩次，兩次之間大約有一到二秒的間隔。聽完兩次後，請馬上回答，每題回答時間爲 15 秒，請在作答時間內儘量的表達。

1. **Q** : You see a handbag that you like in a market. It costs 500 dollars. Ask for a discount.

   你在市場裡看到一個你喜歡的手提袋。它需要五百塊錢。要求對方折扣。

   **A1** : "This bag is nice, but it's too expensive. It's not worth 500. I'll give you 450 for it. What do you say?" 「這個袋子眞不錯，但它太貴了。它不值五百元。我給你四百五十元買它。你覺得如何？」

   **A2** : "I like this bag, but I couldn't possibly pay 500. That's too much. What's your best price?" 「我喜歡這個袋子，但是我不可能付五百元。那太多了。你最低的價格是多少？」

   【註】 handbag (ˈhændˌbæg ) *n.* 手提袋
   market (ˈmɑrkɪt ) *n.* 市場　　cost ( kɔst ) *v.* 需要…錢
   ***ask for*** 要求　　discount (ˈdɪskaunt ) *n.* 折扣
   nice ( naɪs ) *adj.* 好的　　worth ( wɜθ ) *adj.* 值得…的
   possibly (ˈpɑsəblɪ ) *adv.* 可能　　pay ( pe ) *v.* 付
   best ( bɛst ) *adj.* 最好的　　price ( praɪs ) *n.* 價格
   ***What's your best price?*** 你最低的價格是多少？

**A3**："I'll take this bag if you can lower the price. How much of a discount can you offer?  Let's make a deal."

「如果你能降低價格，我就買這個袋子。你能提供多少折扣呢？讓我們達成交易吧。」

~~~~~~~~~~~~~~~~~~~~~~~~~~~~~~~~~~~

**2. Q**　：You meet an old friend that you haven't seen for two years.  What do you say to him or her?

你遇到了兩年沒見的老朋友。你會跟他（她）說什麼？

**A1**：I'd say, "Wow!  I can't believe it!  It's been such a long time.  You look great."

我會說：「哇！我真是不敢相信！已經過了這麼久的時間。你看起來好極了。」

【註】　take〔tek〕*v.* 買　　lower〔'loɚ〕*v.* 降低
　　　　offer〔'ɔfɚ〕*v.* 提供　　deal〔dil〕*n.* 交易
　　　　***make a deal*** 達成交易　　meet〔mit〕*v.* 遇見
　　　　old〔old〕*adj.* 舊的；老的
　　　　wow〔waʊ〕*interj.* 哇！　　believe〔bɪ'liv〕*v.* 相信
　　　　such〔sʌtʃ〕*adj.* 如此的　　look〔lʊk〕*v.* 看起來
　　　　great〔gret〕*adj.* 很棒的

**A2**：I'd say, "It's great to see you.  I'm so sorry we lost touch.  Let's go somewhere and have a long chat.  Let's catch up."

我會說：「能遇見你真是太好了。我很難過我們失去了聯絡。讓我們找個地方好好地聊一聊。我們來敘敘舊吧。」

**A3**：I'd say, "How nice to see you again.  What are you doing now?  Tell me everything."

我會說：「再見到你真好。你現在在做什麼呢？把所有的事情都告訴我吧。」

～～～～～～～～～～

**3. Q**：You should hand in some homework to your teacher today, but you left it at home.  What do you say to your teacher?

你今天應該要交一些作業給你的老師，但是你把它留在家裡了。你會向你的老師說什麼？

【註】　sorry (ˈsɔrɪ) *adj.* 感到難過的　　lose (luz) *v.* 失去
touch (tʌtʃ) *n.* 接觸；連繫　***lose touch*** 失去聯絡
somewhere (ˈsʌm͵hwɛr) *adv.* (到) 某處
chat (tʃæt) *n.* 聊天　***catch up*** 敘舊；談談近況
again (əˈgɛn) *adv.* 再一次　***hand in*** 繳交
homework (ˈhom͵wɝk) *n.* 家庭作業
leave (liv) *v.* 遺留

**A1**：I'd say, "I'm sorry I don't have my homework.　I did it last night, but I left it at home.　Could I hand it in tomorrow?"

我會說：「我很抱歉，我沒帶我的作業。我昨晚做好了，但我把它留在家裡了。我能明天再交嗎？」

**A2**：I'd say, "I'm afraid I don't have it.　I finished it, but I forgot to bring it to school.　Please believe me!"

我會說：「恐怕我沒帶我的作業。我做完了，但是我忘記帶來學校。請相信我！」

**A3**：I'd say, "Unfortunately, my assignment is at home.　I'm so sorry for my mistake.　I'll bring it to you tomorrow morning."

我會說：「很遺憾，我的作業在家裡。對於我的錯誤我很抱歉。我明天早上會帶來給你。」

---

**4. Q**：Imagine you lent 1,000 dollars to your friend last week.　He promised to pay you back in three days, but he didn't.　What would you do?

想像一下，上週你借給朋友一千塊錢。他保證三天內會還給你，但是他沒有。你會怎麼做？

【註】　afraid ( əˈfred ) *adj.* 恐怕⋯的　　finish (ˈfɪnɪʃ ) *v.* 完成
　　　　unfortunately ( ʌnˈfɔrtʃənɪtlɪ ) *adv.* 不幸地；遺憾地
　　　　assignment ( əˈsaɪnmənt ) *n.* 作業；功課
　　　　mistake ( məˈstek ) *n.* 錯誤
　　　　imagine ( ɪˈmædʒɪn ) *v.* 想像　　lend ( lɛnd ) *v.* 借 ( 出 )
　　　　promise (ˈprɑmɪs ) *v.* 保證　　***pay sb. back*** 還某人錢

**A1**：I would ask him about it.  I would say, "Do you remember that thousand I lent you last week?  Are you able to pay me back now?"
我會問問他這件事。我會說：「你記得我上週借你的一千塊嗎？你現在可以還我錢了嗎？」

**A2**：I think I would wait a few more days.  Maybe he doesn't have the money and is embarrassed.  Even if he never pays me back, it's OK.  Friends are more important than money.
我想我會多等幾天。也許他沒有錢，而且經濟拮据。即使他永遠不還我，也沒關係。朋友比錢更重要。

**A3**：I would drop some hints.  I would talk about something I wanted to buy and then say, "Oh, but I don't have enough money now."  Maybe it would make him remember.　我會做點暗示。我會談論某個我想要買的東西，然後說：「哦，但是我現在沒有足夠的錢。」也許這會讓他想起來。

【註】　*ask sb. about sth.* 詢問某人關於某事
　　　　thousand (ˈθaʊznd) *n.* 千
　　　　*be able to V.* 能夠　　*a few* 一些；幾個
　　　　embarrassed ( ɪmˈbærəst ) *adj.* 尷尬的；金錢窘迫的
　　　　*even if* 即使　　never (ˈnɛvɚ) *adv.* 從不
　　　　OK (ˈoˈke) *adj.* 沒問題的
　　　　important ( ɪmˈpɔrtn̩t ) *adj.* 重要的
　　　　drop ( drɑp ) *v.* 偶然說出　　hint ( hɪnt ) *n.* 提示
　　　　*drop a hint* 做暗示　　oh ( o ) *interj.* 哦
　　　　enough ( əˈnʌf ) *adj.* 足夠的　　make ( mek ) *v.* 使
　　　　remember ( rɪˈmɛmbɚ ) *v.* 想起；記得

**5. Q** ：You have a doctor's appointment at 10:00.  You want to change the time to 3:00.  What do you say when you call the doctor's office?

你十點跟醫生有約。你想要把時間改到三點。當你打電話到醫生的診所時，你會說什麼？

**A1**：I'd say, "This is John Smith.  I have a 10:00 appointment with Dr. Brown.  I'm afraid I can't make it then.  Would it be possible to come this afternoon at 3:00?"

我會說：「我是約翰史密斯。我十點鐘跟布朗醫生有約。那個時間我恐怕不能去。可能改成今天下午三點嗎？」

**A2**：I'd say, "Good morning.  I need to change my appointment with Dr. Brown.  I can't come in this morning.  Is he free at 3:00?"

我會說：「早安。我需要更改我跟布朗醫生的約診。我今天早上沒辦法去。請問他三點有空嗎？」

【註】　appointment〔ə'pɔɪntmənt〕*n.* 約會；約診
change〔tʃendʒ〕*v.* 更改　　call〔kɔl〕*v.* 打電話給
office〔'ɔfɪs〕*n.* 診所　　Smith〔smɪθ〕*n.* 史密斯
Dr.〔'dɑktɚ〕*n.* 醫生（= *doctor*）
Brown〔braʊn〕*n.* 布朗　　***make it*** 能去
possible〔'pɑsəbl〕*adj.* 可能的
need〔nid〕*v.* 必須　　free〔fri〕*adj.* 有空的

**A3**: I'd say, "Hello. I'm supposed to see Dr. Brown at 10:00 but I have to cancel the appointment. Can we reschedule for 3:00 today?" 我會說：「哈囉。我今天十點鐘應該要給布朗醫生看診的，但我必須取消預約。我們能重新安排在今天的三點嗎？」

---

**6. Q** : You want to borrow your parents' car to drive your friends to a movie theater. What do you say? 你想要借你父母的車，載你的朋友去電影院。你會怎麼說？

**A1**: I will say, "Mom and Dad, can I borrow the car? My friends and I are going to a movie. We'll be back by 10:00. I'll be very careful."
我會說：「爸、媽，我能借車子嗎？我跟我朋友要去看電影。我們會在十點前回來。我會非常小心的。」

【註】 hello ( həˋlo ) *interj.* 哈囉
　　　 *be suppose to V.* 應該… 　　　 cancel (ˋkænsḷ ) *v.* 取消
　　　 reschedule ( riˋskɛdʒul ) *v.* 重新安排時間
　　　 borrow (ˋbɑro ) *v.* 借（入）
　　　 parents (ˋpɛrənts ) *n. pl.* 父母
　　　 drive ( draɪv ) *v.* 開車載（人）　　　 movie (ˋmuvɪ ) *n.* 電影
　　　 theater (ˋθiətɚ ) *n.* 戲院　　　 *movie theater* 電影院
　　　 mom ( mɑm ) *n.* 媽媽　　　 dad ( dæd ) *n.* 爸爸
　　　 *go to a movie* 去看電影　　　 *be back* 回來
　　　 by ( baɪ ) *prep.* 在…之前　　　 careful (ˋkɛrfəl ) *adj.* 小心的

**A2**：I will say, "Could I use the car tonight?　I'm going out with my friends and it's my turn to drive.　It would really help us out a lot."

我會說：「我今晚能用車嗎？我要跟我的朋友出去，而且這次輪到我開車。這真的會幫我們很大的忙。」

**A3**：I will say, "May I borrow the car to go to the movies?　I'll drive straight to the cinema and then straight home.　You can trust me."

我會說：「我可以借車子開去看電影嗎？我會直接開去電影院，然後直接開回家。你們可以信任我。」

---

**7. Q**　：You have to finish your math homework, but you don't know how to do it.　Ask your older brother or sister for help.　你必須完成你的數學作業，但是你不知道怎麼做。向你的哥哥或姊姊尋求幫助。

【註】　use〔juz〕v. 使用　　***go out*** 外出
turn〔tɜn〕n. 輪流順序　　***it's my turn to V.*** 輪到我做…
***help out*** 幫助　　***a lot*** 許多
***go to the movies*** 去看電影　　drive〔draɪv〕v. 開車
straight〔stret〕adv. 直接地
cinema〔'sɪnəmə〕n. 電影院　　trust〔trʌst〕v. 信任
***have to*** 必須　　finish〔'fɪnɪʃ〕v. 完成
math〔mæθ〕n. 數學　　***ask sb. for help*** 向某人求助

**A1** : I'd say, "Do you have time to help me? I can't figure this math problem out. Can you show me how to do it?" 我會說:「你有時間幫我嗎?我不會解這個數學題。你能教我怎麼做嗎?」

**A2** : I'd say, "Can you help me with my homework? You're so good at math, and I just don't get it. I'd really appreciate it."

我會說:「你能教我寫我的數學作業嗎?你對數學這麼擅長,而我就是無法了解它。我真的會很感激你的。」

**A3** : I'd say, "Do you know how to do these problems? Can you explain it to me? I really need your help."

我會說:「你知道怎麼算這些問題嗎?你能解釋給我聽嗎?我真的需要你的幫忙。」

【註】 *figure out* 算出;了解　　problem (ˈprɑbləm ) *n.* 問題
show ( ʃo ) *v.* 使…明白　　so ( so ) *adv.* 如此地
*be good at* 擅長　　*get it* 了解
appreciate ( əˈpriʃɪˌet ) *v.* 感激　　do ( du ) *v.* 做;解開
explain ( ɪkˈsplen ) *v.* 解釋　　need ( nid ) *v.* 需要

\* 請將下列自我介紹的句子再唸一遍,請開始:

My seat number is (複試座位號碼) , and my test number is

(初試准考證號碼).

# 初級英語檢定測驗第二階段

# 寫作口說能力測驗④

## 寫作能力測驗

　　本測驗共有兩部份。第一部份為單句寫作，第二部份為段落寫作。測驗時間為 40 分鐘。

### 第一部份：單句寫作

　　請將答案寫在答案紙上對應的題號旁，如有文法、用字、拼字、標點符號、大小寫等之錯誤，將予扣分。

### 第 1～5 題：句子改寫

　　請依題目之提示，將原句依指定型式改寫，並將改寫的句子<u>完整</u>地寫在答案紙上。

　　注意：須寫出提示之文字及標點符號。

例：　題目：I am fine.

　　　She ＿＿＿＿＿＿.

　　在答案紙上寫：***She is fine.***

1. I'm playing volleyball this Saturday.

　 I usually ＿＿＿＿＿＿＿＿＿＿＿＿＿＿ on Saturdays.

2. My sister gave me her notebook.

　 I took ＿＿＿＿＿＿＿＿＿＿＿＿＿＿＿＿.

3. George drove his car to Kenting.

Where _____?

4. When will the bus come?

Do you know _____?

5. I can't swim and neither can Tim.

Neither _____ nor _____.

第 6～10 題：句子合併

請依照題目指示，將兩句合併成一句。並將合併的句子完整地寫在答案紙上。

注意：須寫出提示之文字及標點符號。

例： 題目： John has a cap.

The cap is purple.

John _____ cap.

在答案紙上寫： ***John has a purple cap.***

6. Lisa saw a lion at the zoo.

Lisa saw a tiger at the zoo.

Lisa saw _____.

7. We listened to the radio.

We were painting the living room.

While painting _____.

8. I will eat fried noodles.

I will eat pizza.

I will eat _____ or _____.

9. Susan painted the picture.

The picture is hanging in the living room.

Susan _____.

10. I missed the bus to school.

I will take a taxi.

I _____, so _____.

第 11～15 題：重組

請將題目中所有提示的字詞整合成一有意義的句子，並將重組的句子完整地寫在答案紙上。

注意： 須寫出提示之文字及標點符號。（答案中必須使用所有提示的字詞，且不能隨意增減字詞，否則不予計分。）

例： 題目：John _____.

this morning / late / was / again

在答案紙上寫：***John was late again this morning.***

11. Did _____?

will / what time / you / the train / hear / leave

12. I _____.

the weather report / the volume / could / so that / turned up /

I / hear

13. Terry _____.

his school / runner / is / in / the / fastest

14. I studied _____.

still / failed / the test / hard / but / for / I / ,

15. You _____?

didn't / the letter / you / wrote / ,

## 第二部份：段落寫作

題目：昨天，瑪麗（Mary）去逛街買衣服。沒想到試穿的
時候，有奇怪的東西在衣服裡面。請根據圖片內容
寫一篇約 50 字的簡短描述。

# 口說能力測驗

＊請在 15 秒內完成並唸出下列自我介紹的句子，請開始：

My seat number is (複試座位號碼) , and my test number is (初試准考證號碼) .

## I. 複誦

共五題。題目不印在試題上，由耳機播出，每題播出兩次，兩次之間大約有一到二秒的間隔。聽完兩次後，請馬上複誦一次。

## II. 朗讀句子與短文

共有五個句子及一篇短文，請先利用一分鐘的時間閱讀試題上的句子與短文，然後在一分鐘內以正常的速度，清楚正確的朗讀一遍。

One　　: I havc to go to a piano class on Wednesday.

Two　　: My dog likes to sleep on that chair because it is comfortable.

Three　: This is too much food for one person!

Four　 : How much did you pay for your shoes?

Five　 : I don't like her hairstyle at all.

Six : The party was a big success. Jack was really surprised. He had no idea we were planning a party. Of course, all of his friends came, and everyone brought a present. We also ordered a lot of food and a big cake. The cake was chocolate, because that's Jack's favorite. I hope my birthday party is as much fun.

## III. 回答問題

共七題。題目不印在試題上，由耳機播出，每題播出兩次，兩次之間大約有一到二秒的間隔。聽完兩次後，請馬上回答，每題回答時間為 15 秒，請在作答時間內儘量的表達。

＊請將下列自我介紹的句子再唸一遍，請開始：

My seat number is （複試座位號碼）, and my test number is （初試准考證號碼）.

# 寫作口說能力測驗 ④ 詳解

## 寫作能力測驗詳解

**第一部份：單句寫作**

第 1~5 題：句子改寫

1. I'm playing volleyball this Saturday.

   I usually ＿＿＿＿＿＿＿＿＿＿＿＿＿＿＿ on Saturdays.

     **重點結構：**頻率副詞的用法

      **解　答：**I usually play volleyball on Saturdays.

     **句型分析：**主詞＋頻率副詞＋一般動詞＋時間副詞

      **說　明：**usually（通常）為頻率副詞，須放在助動詞之後，或一般動詞之前，主詞 I 為第一人稱單數，故動詞 playing volleyball 須改為 play volleyball。

     \* play〔ple〕v. 打（球）　　volleyball〔'vɑlɪ,bɔl〕n. 排球
     ***on Saturdays*** 在星期六；每星期六

2. My sister gave me her notebook.

   I took ＿＿＿＿＿＿＿＿＿＿＿＿＿＿＿＿＿.

     **重點結構：**句子基本結構

      **解　答：**I took my sister's notebook.

     **句型分析：**主詞＋動詞＋受詞

      **說　明：**這題的意思是說「我姐姐給我她的筆記本」，換句話說，就是「我拿了我姐姐的筆記本」，用 take（拿）改寫。

     \* notebook〔'not,bʊk〕n. 筆記本

3. George drove his car to Kenting.

   Where _____?

   重點結構：肯定句改爲疑問句

   解　答：<u>Where did George drive his car?</u>

   句型分析：Where + 助動詞 + 主詞 + 動詞？

   說　明：這一題將過去式直述句改爲 where 問句，除了要用
   　　　　助動詞 did，還要將助動詞後面的動詞改爲原形動
   　　　　詞，因此 drove 改成 drive。

   \* drive〔draɪv〕v. 開（車）　　***Kenting*** 墾丁

4. When will the bus come?

   Do you know _____?

   重點結構：直接問句改爲間接問句

   解　答：<u>Do you know when the bus will come?</u>

   句型分析：Do you know + when + 主詞 + 動詞？

   說　明：Do you know 後面須接受詞，故直接問句 When
   　　　　will the bus come? 須改爲間接問句當受詞，即「疑
   　　　　問詞 + 主詞 + 動詞」的形式。

5. I can't swim and neither can Tim.

   Neither _____ nor _____.

   重點結構：「neither…nor～」的用法

   解　答：<u>Neither Tim nor I can swim.</u>

   　或：<u>Neither I nor Tim can swim.</u>

   句型分析：Neither + A + nor + B + 助動詞 + 原形動詞

說　明：「neither…nor～」爲對等連接詞，用來連接文法
　　　　作用相同的單字、片語或子句，本身已有否定的意
　　　　思，故後面接肯定的句型。句意爲，「我和提姆都不
　　　　會游泳」。

* swim〔swɪm〕v. 游泳

## 第6～10題：句子合併

6. Lisa saw a lion at the zoo.
   Lisa saw a tiger at the zoo.
   Lisa saw _____.

　　重點結構：and 的用法
　　　解　答：Lisa saw a lion and a tiger at the zoo.
　　句型分析：主詞＋動詞＋A＋and＋B＋地方副詞
　　　說　明：連接詞 and（和）爲對等連接詞，連接前後文法功
　　　　　　　能相同的單字、片語或句子，此題的 and 連接二個
　　　　　　　名詞，即 a lion 和 a tiger。

* lion〔'laɪən〕n. 獅子　　zoo〔zu〕n. 動物園
  tiger〔'taɪgɚ〕n. 老虎

7. We listened to the radio.
   We were painting the living room.
   While painting _____.

　　重點結構：while 的用法
　　　解　答：While painting the living room, we listened to
　　　　　　　the radio.

句型分析：While＋動詞（進行式）＋, ＋主詞＋動詞（過去式）

說　明：while（當…的時候）後面接的副詞子句，通常是
持續一段時間的動作，故常用進行式，即 while
子句是一條「時間線」，而主要子句是這條線上的
一個「時間點」，故常用過去式。while 子句若放在
主要子句前，兩句之間須加一逗點，反之則否。

* **listen to** 聽　　radio〔'redɪ,o〕*n.* 無線電廣播
paint〔pent〕*v.* 油漆　　***living room*** 客廳

8. I will eat fried noodles.

I will eat pizza.

I will eat ＿＿＿＿＿＿＿＿＿ or ＿＿＿＿＿＿＿＿＿.

重點結構：or 的用法

解　答：<u>I will eat fried noodles or pizza.</u>
　　　或 <u>I will eat pizza or fried noodles.</u>

句型分析：主詞＋動詞＋A＋or＋B

說　明：連接詞 or（或者）為選擇連接詞，連接兩個文法功
能相同的單字、片語或句子，而在其中選擇一個，
本句的意思是，「我將會吃炒麵或披薩」。

* fried〔fraɪd〕*adj.* 油炸的；炒的　　noodle〔'nudl̩〕*n.* 麵條
***fried noodles*** 炒麵　　pizza〔'pitsə〕*n.* 披薩

9. Susan painted the picture.

The picture is hanging in the living room.

Susan ＿＿＿＿＿＿＿＿＿＿＿＿＿＿＿＿＿＿.

重點結構：形容詞子句的用法

解　答：<u>Susan painted the picture (that/which is)</u>
　　　　<u>hanging in the living room.</u>

句型分析：主詞＋動詞＋受詞＋（that/which）＋形容詞子句

說　明：本題的意思是「掛在客廳的那幅畫是蘇珊畫的」，
　　　　在合併兩句時，用關係代名詞 that 或 which 代替
　　　　先行詞 the picture，在子句中做主詞，引導形容
　　　　詞子句，又形容詞子句中的關代和 be 動詞可同時
　　　　省略，故 that/which is 可省略不寫。

＊ paint〔pent〕v. 畫（畫）　　picture〔'pɪktʃɚ〕n. 圖畫
　 hang〔hæŋ〕v. 懸掛

10. I missed the bus to school.

I will take a taxi.

I ＿＿＿＿＿＿＿＿＿＿＿＿＿, so ＿＿＿＿＿＿＿＿＿＿＿＿＿.

重點結構：so 的用法

解　答：<u>I missed the bus to school, so I will take a taxi.</u>

句型分析：主詞＋動詞＋, ＋ so ＋主詞＋動詞

說　明：連接詞 so（所以）和 because（因為）的比較：
　　　　$\begin{cases} 原因 + , so + 結果 \\ 結果 + because + 原因 \end{cases}$
　　　　原因是「我錯過了去學校的巴士」，結果是「我將
　　　　會搭計程車」，把原因放在 so 之前，結果放在 so
　　　　之後。

＊ miss〔mɪs〕v. 錯過　　take〔tek〕v. 搭乘（交通工具）
　 taxi〔'tæksɪ〕n. 計程車

第 11～15 題：重組

11. Did _____?

will / what time / you / the train / hear / leave

  重點結構：名詞子句的用法

   解　答：<u>Did you hear what time the train will leave?</u>

  句型分析：Did you hear + what time + 主詞 + 動詞？

   説　明：Did you hear 後面少了受詞，用 what time 引導的
      名詞子句做受詞，即「疑問詞＋主詞＋動詞」的形
      式，因名詞子句非問句，故該主詞與動詞不需倒裝。

  * train ( tren ) *n.* 火車　　leave ( liv ) *v.* 離開

12. I _____.

the weather report / the volume / could / so that / turned up /

I / hear

  重點結構：so that 的用法

   解　答：<u>I turned up the volume so that I could hear the</u>
      <u>weather report.</u>

  句型分析：主詞 + 動詞 + so that + 主詞 + can/could/may
      /might/will/would + 原形動詞

   説　明：so that（以便；為了）是一表「目的」的從屬連接
      詞，其所引導的副詞子句中，必須要有如上列的助
      動詞之一，且該子句只能放在主要子句之後。句意
      為，「我把音量開大，以便聽氣象報告。」

  * *turn up* 將…開大聲　　volume ('valjəm ) *n.* 音量
  weather ('wɛðɚ ) *n.* 天氣　　report ( rɪ'port ) *n.* 報告
  *weather report* 氣象報告

13. Terry ＿＿＿＿＿＿＿＿＿＿＿＿＿＿＿＿＿＿＿＿.

　　his school / runner / is / in / the / fastest

　　　重點結構：最高級的用法

　　　解　　答：<u>Terry is the fastest runner in his school.</u>

　　　句型分析：主詞＋be 動詞＋the＋最高級形容詞＋名詞＋
　　　　　　　　地方副詞

　　　說　　明：本題的意思是，「泰瑞在他的學校裡是跑得最快的
　　　　　　　　跑者」，用最高級表達，即「the＋最高級形容詞＋
　　　　　　　　名詞」，先找出 be 動詞 is，後面接 the fastest
　　　　　　　　runner，in his school 為地方副詞，放在句尾。

　　　* fast〔fæst〕*adj.* 快速的　　　runner〔'rʌnɚ〕*n.* 跑者


14. I studied ＿＿＿＿＿＿＿＿＿＿＿＿＿＿＿＿＿＿＿.

　　still / failed / the test / hard / but / for / I / ,

　　　重點結構：but 的用法

　　　解　　答：<u>I studied hard for the test, but I still failed.</u>

　　　句型分析：主詞＋動詞＋副詞＋for the test＋,＋but＋主詞
　　　　　　　　＋副詞＋動詞

　　　說　　明：依句意，「我為了考試而用功唸書，但我還是考不及
　　　　　　　　格」，用反義連接詞 but，來連接前後所說的意義恰
　　　　　　　　好相反或相互對比的句子。

　　　* ***study hard*** 用功讀書　　　test〔tɛst〕*n.* 測驗；考試
　　　　 still〔stɪl〕*adv.* 仍然　　　　fail〔fel〕*v.*（考試）不及格

15. You _____?

   didn't / the letter / you / wrote / ,

   **重點結構**：附加問句的用法

   **解　　答**：<u>You wrote the letter, didn't you?</u>

   **句型分析**：主詞＋動詞（肯定）＋，＋助動詞否定的縮寫＋
   人稱代名詞？

   **說　　明**：句首非疑問詞或助動詞，且句尾是問號，故本題後
   應有附加問句，句意為：「你寫信了，不是嗎？」

   \* letter〔'lɛtɚ〕*n.* 信

## 第二部份：段落寫作

【作文範例】

*Yesterday* Mary went shopping. She found a beautiful
dress. She tried it on. Suddenly, Mary felt something
crawling on her skin. There was something strange inside the
dress! Mary jumped and screamed. A salesgirl came inside
the dressing room. She found an insect in the dress. Mary
was very scared, but the salesgirl killed the insect.

   \* shop〔ʃɑp〕*v.* 購物　　dress〔drɛs〕*n.* 洋裝　　*try on* 試穿
   suddenly〔'sʌdṇlɪ〕*adv.* 突然地　　crawl〔krɔl〕*v.* 爬行
   skin〔skɪn〕*n.* 皮膚　　strange〔strendʒ〕*adj.* 奇怪的
   inside〔ɪn'saɪd〕*prep.* 在…裡面　　jump〔dʒʌmp〕*v.* 跳
   scream〔skrim〕*v.* 尖叫　　salesgirl〔'selz,gɜl〕*n.* 女店員
   *dressing room* 更衣室　　insect〔'ɪnsɛkt〕*n.* 昆蟲
   scared〔skɛrd〕*adj.* 害怕的　　kill〔kɪl〕*v.* 殺死

# 口說能力測驗詳解

＊請在15秒內完成並唸出下列自我介紹的句子，請開始：

My seat number is （複試座位號碼）, and my test number is （初試准考證號碼）.

## I. 複誦

共五題。題目不印在試題上，由耳機播出，每題播出兩次，兩次之間大約有一到二秒的間隔。聽完兩次後，請馬上複誦一次。

1. It's going to rain tomorrow.　明天將會下雨。

2. My glasses are on the table.　我的眼鏡在桌上。

3. The elevator is out of order.　電梯故障了。

4. Mary is sick today.　瑪莉今天生病了。

5. Do you know how to swim?　你知道如何游泳嗎？

【註】 *be going to V.* 將會…　　rain〔ren〕*v.* 下雨
glasses〔'glæsɪz〕*n. pl.* 眼鏡
table〔'tebḷ〕*n.* 桌子
elevator〔'ɛlə,vetɚ〕*n.* 電梯
*out of order* 故障　　sick〔sɪk〕*adj.* 生病的
swim〔swɪm〕*v.* 游泳

## II. 朗讀句子與短文

共有五個句子及一篇短文,請先利用一分鐘的時間閱讀試題上的句子與短文,然後在一分鐘內以正常的速度,清楚正確的朗讀一遍。

**One** : I have to go to a piano class on Wednesday.
我星期三必須去上鋼琴課。

**Two** : My dog likes to sleep on that chair because it is comfortable.
我的狗喜歡在那張椅子上睡覺,因為椅子很舒服。

**Three** : This is too much food for one person!
這些食物對一個人來說太多了!

**Four** : How much did you pay for your shoes?
你花了多少錢買你的鞋子?

**Five** : I don't like her hairstyle at all.
我一點也不喜歡她的髮型。

【註】 *have to* 必須　　piano〔pɪˋæno〕*n.* 鋼琴
class〔klæs〕*n.* 課程
Wednesday〔ˋwɛnzde〕*n.* 星期三
like〔laɪk〕*v.* 喜歡　　sleep〔slip〕*v.* 睡覺
chair〔tʃɛr〕*n.* 椅子
comfortable〔ˋkʌmfətəbḷ〕*adj.* 舒適的
*too much* 太多　　food〔fud〕*n.* 食物
person〔ˋpɝsṇ〕*n.* 人　　*pay for* 支付…的錢
shoe〔ʃu〕*n.* 鞋子　　hairstyle〔ˋhɛr͵staɪl〕*n.* 髮型
*not…at all* 一點也不…

Six：The party was a big success. Jack was really surprised. He had no idea we were planning a party. Of course, all of his friends came, and everyone brought a present. We also ordered a lot of food and a big cake. The cake was chocolate, because that's Jack's favorite. I hope my birthday party is as much fun.

這個派對非常成功。傑克真的很驚訝。他不知道我們策劃了一個派對。當然,他所有的朋友都來了,而且每個人都帶了禮物。我們也訂了很多食物和一個大蛋糕。蛋糕是巧克力的,因為那是傑克最喜歡的口味。我希望我的生日派對能和他的一樣有趣。

【註】 party ('partɪ) n. 宴會;派對
　　　 success ( sək'sɛs ) n. 成功　　Jack ( dʒæk ) n. 傑克
　　　 really ('rɪəlɪ) adv. 真地
　　　 surprised ( sə'praɪzd ) adj. 驚訝的
　　　 idea ( aɪ'diə ) n. 概念　　*have no idea* 不知道
　　　 plan ( plæn ) v. 計畫　　*of course* 當然
　　　 bring ( brɪŋ ) v. 帶來　　present ('prɛznt ) n. 禮物
　　　 also ('ɔlso ) adv. 也　　order ('ɔrdə ) v. 訂購
　　　 *a lot of* 許多的　　cake ( kek ) n. 蛋糕
　　　 chocolate ('tʃɔklɪt ) adj. 巧克力的
　　　 favorite ('fevərɪt ) n. 最喜愛的事物
　　　 hope ( hop ) v. 希望　　birthday ('bɝθ,de ) n. 生日
　　　 *as much* 一樣多;那麼多　　fun ( fʌn ) n. 樂趣

## Ⅲ. 回答問題

共七題。題目不印在試題上，由耳機播出，每題播出兩次，兩次之間大約有一到二秒的間隔。聽完兩次後，請馬上回答，每題回答時間為15秒，請在作答時間內儘量的表達。

**1. Q** : Imagine you are returning a book to the library. It is one week overdue. What do you say to the librarian? 想像一下，你正在還一本書給圖書館。那本書已經逾期一週了。你會對圖書館員說什麼？

**A1** : "Here is a book I borrowed last month. I'm sorry it's late. How much do I have to pay?"
「這是我上個月借的書。我很抱歉我逾期了。我需要付多少錢？」

**A2** : "I checked out this book a while ago. It was due last week, but I forgot to bring it back. Do I have to pay a fine?" 「我不久之前借了這本書。這本書上週到期，但是我忘記把它拿來還了。請問我需要繳罰金嗎？」

【註】 imagine〔ɪˈmædʒɪn〕v. 想像　　return〔rɪˈtɜn〕v. 歸還
library〔ˈlaɪˌbrɛrɪ〕n. 圖書館　　week〔wik〕n. 週
overdue〔ˈovɚˈdju〕adj. 逾期的
librarian〔laɪˈbrɛrɪən〕n. 圖書館員
borrow〔ˈbaro〕v. 借（入）　　*last month* 上個月
late〔let〕adj. 遲的；晚的　　*check out* 借出
*a while ago* 不久之前　　due〔dju〕adj. 到期的
*last week* 上週　　forget〔fɚˈgɛt〕v. 忘記
*bring back* 歸還　　pay〔pe〕v. 支付
fine〔faɪn〕n. 罰金

**A3**："I'm sorry to return this book late.  I completely forgot about the due date.  I promise that it won't happen again."　「很抱歉我太晚還這本書。我完全忘記到期日。我保證不會再發生這種事了。」

---

**2. Q**：You are ordering a set meal in a restaurant.  It comes with French fries, but you want a salad instead.  What do you say?
你正在餐廳點一份套餐。那份套餐搭配的是薯條，但是你想要換成沙拉。你會說什麼？

**A1**：I would say, "I'd like to order the special.  But I don't eat French fries.  Could I have a small salad instead?"　我會說：「我想要點特餐。但是我不吃薯條。我能換成一份小的沙拉嗎？」

【註】 completely ( kəm'plitlı ) adv. 完全地
date ( det ) n. 日期　　*due date* 到期日
promise ('prɑmıs ) v. 保證　　happen ('hæpən ) v. 發生
again ( ə'gɛn ) adv. 再　　order ('ɔrdə ) v. 點 ( 餐 )
set ( sɛt ) n. 一套；一組　　meal ( mil ) n. 一餐
*set meal* 套餐　　restaurant ('rɛstərənt ) n. 餐廳
*come with* 伴隨　　*French fries* 薯條
salad ('sæləd ) n. 沙拉
instead ( ın'stɛd ) adv. 作為代替
*would like* 想要　　special ('spɛʃəl ) n. 特餐

**A2**：I would say, "I want the lunch special, but I don't want French fries.  Can I substitute something else?  Can I have a salad?"

我會說：「我想要中午的特餐，但是我不想要薯條。我能用別的東西代替嗎？我可不可以要一份沙拉？」

**A3**：I would say, "Can you make the lunch special with a salad instead of fries?  I really don't want any fries.  I'd appreciate it."

我會說：「你們能做一份附沙拉而不是薯條的中午特餐嗎？我眞的不想要任何薯條。我會很感激的。」

───────〰〰〰───────

**3. Q**　：You are sitting on the train and a man nearby starts smoking.  Smoking is not allowed and you want him to stop.  What would you do?

你正坐在火車上，附近有一個男人開始抽煙。抽煙是不被允許的，而你希望他停止抽煙。你會怎麼做？

**【註】**　lunch〔lʌntʃ〕*n.* 午餐
　　　　substitute〔'sʌbstə,tjut〕*v.* 用～代替
　　　　***something else*** 其他東西　　make〔mek〕*v.* 做
　　　　fries〔fraɪz〕*n. pl.* 薯條（= *French fries*）
　　　　appreciate〔ə'priʃɪ,et〕*v.* 感激
　　　　train〔tren〕*n.* 火車　　nearby〔'nɪr'baɪ〕*adv.* 在附近
　　　　start〔stɑrt〕*v.* 開始　　smoke〔smok〕*v.* 抽煙
　　　　smoking〔'smokɪŋ〕*n.* 抽煙　　allow〔ə'lau〕*v.* 允許
　　　　stop〔stɑp〕*v.* 停止

**A1** : I would talk to him politely. I would tell him that
smoking is not allowed on the train. If he didn't
put out his cigarette, I would call the conductor.
我會很客氣地跟他說話。我會告訴他,火車上是不允許
抽煙的。如果他不熄滅他的香煙的話,我會請列車長來。

**A2** : I wouldn't say anything to him. I would just move
to a different car. But if there were no other seats,
then I would say, "Please don't smoke here."
我不會對他說任何話。我會直接到另一個車廂。但是如
果那裡沒有其他位子的話,那麼我會說:「請不要在這
裡吸煙。」

**A3** : I would tell the conductor. It's his job to enforce
the rules. I would tell him, "There is someone
smoking on the train. Would you please ask him
to put out his cigarette?"
我會告訴列車長。實行規定是他的工作。我會告訴他:
「有人在火車上吸煙。能不能請你去要求他把香煙熄掉?」

【註】 politely ( pə'laɪtlɪ ) *adv.* 客氣地;有禮貌地
***put out*** 熄滅　　cigarette ('sɪgə,rɛt ) *n.* 香煙
call ( kɔl ) *v.* 叫來　　conductor ( kən'dʌktə ) *n.* 列車長
move ( muv ) *v.* 移動;前進
different ('dɪfərənt ) *adj.* 不同的　　car ( kɑr ) *n.* 車廂
other ('ʌðə ) *adj.* 其他的　　seat ( sit ) *n.* 座位
then ( ðɛn ) *adv.* 那麼　　job ( dʒɑb ) *n.* 工作;職責
enforce ( ɪn'fors ) *v.* 執行;實施　　rule ( rul ) *n.* 規定

**4. Q**： You have a date at a coffee shop with a friend.
You arrive 20 minutes late.  What do you say to
your friend?　你和你的朋友約在咖啡廳見面。你晚
了二十分鐘才抵達。你會對你的朋友說什麼？

**A1**： I would say, "I'm so sorry I'm late!  Please forgive
me.  It won't happen again."
我會說：「很抱歉我遲到了！請原諒我。不會再發生
這種事了。」

**A2**： I would say, "I know I'm late.  Let me make it up
to you.  The coffee is on me."
我會說：「我知道我遲到了。讓我補償你吧。咖啡我
請客。」

**A3**： I would say, "I'm sorry I kept you waiting.  I hope
you're not mad.  This is really my fault."
我會說：「很抱歉讓你久等了。我希望你沒有生氣。
這真的是我的錯。」

【註】 date〔det〕*n.* 約會　　coffee〔ˈkɔfɪ〕*n.* 咖啡
*coffee shop* 咖啡廳　　arrive〔əˈraɪv〕*v.* 抵達
forgive〔fəˈgɪv〕*v.* 原諒
*make it up to sb.* 補償某人
on〔ɑn〕*prep.* 由…請客　　keep〔kip〕*v.* 使…持續
wait〔wet〕*v.* 等待　　mad〔mæd〕*adj.* 生氣的
fault〔fɔlt〕*n.* 過錯

**5. Q** : You want to go to the museum, but you don't know which bus to take. A bus arrives. Ask the driver for help.

你想要去博物館，但是你不知道該搭哪班公車。有輛公車來了。請司機幫忙。

**A1** : I'd say, "Hello. Does this bus go to the museum? Can you tell me which one does?"

我會說：「哈囉。請問這輛公車有到博物館嗎？你能告訴我哪一班公車有到？」

**A2** : I'd say, "Hi. I'm trying to get to the museum. Is this the correct bus?"

我會說：「嗨。我想去博物館。請問這是正確的公車嗎？」

**A3** : I'd say, "Excuse me. Do you go to the museum? Would you tell me when I should get off?"

我會說：「不好意思。請問你有到博物館嗎？你能告訴我什麼時候該下車嗎？」

【註】 museum〔mju'ziəm〕 *n.* 博物館
take〔tek〕 *v.* 搭乘　　***ask sb. for help*** 請某人幫忙
driver〔'draɪvɚ〕 *n.* 司機
hello〔hə'lo〕 *interj.* 哈囉　　hi〔haɪ〕 *interj.* 嗨
***try to V.*** 想要…；設法…　　***get to*** 到達
correct〔kə'rɛkt〕 *adj.* 正確的　　***get off*** 下車

**6. Q** ：You have a stain on your jacket.  You take it to
a dry cleaner.  Explain the situation.

你的夾克上有一塊污漬。你拿著夾克去乾洗店。

說明一下這個情況。

**A1**：I'd say, "Hi.  I need to get this jacket cleaned.
There is a stain here on the sleeve.  Do you
think you can get it out?"

我會說：「嗨。我這件夾克需要洗。在袖子這裡有
一塊污漬。你想你能把它弄掉嗎？」

**A2**：I'd say, "This jacket needs cleaning.  There's
a stain right here.  I think it's grease.  Can you
remove it?"

我會說：「這件夾克需要清洗。這裡有一塊污漬。
我想那是油污。你可以把它弄掉嗎？」

【註】 stain〔sten〕n. 污漬　　jacket〔'dʒækɪt〕n. 夾克

take〔tek〕v. 拿　　dry〔draɪ〕adj. 乾的

cleaner〔'klinɚ〕n. 洗衣店　　*dry cleaner* 乾洗店

explain〔ɪk'splen〕v. 解釋；說明

situation〔,sɪtʃʊ'eʃən〕n. 情況

*get sth. cleaned* 把某物用乾淨

sleeve〔sliv〕n. 袖子　　*get sth. out* 把某物除去

clean〔klin〕v. 弄乾淨；清洗

*right here* 就在這裡　　grease〔gris〕n. 油脂

remove〔rɪ'muv〕v. 除去

**A3**：I'd say, "I'd like to drop off this jacket. It needs to be dry cleaned, and there is a stain on the sleeve. Please pay special attention to it."

我會說：「我想洗這件夾克。它需要乾洗，袖子上有一塊污漬。請特別留意。」

---

**7. Q** ：You are going on vacation. You need someone to take care of your dog. How would you ask your friend?

你將要去度假。你需要某人照顧你的狗。你會如何請求你的朋友？

**A1**：I'd say, "Could you do me a big favor? I need someone to watch my dog for a couple of days. Do you think you can do it?"

我會說：「你可以幫我一個大忙嗎？我需要有人看顧我的狗兩、三天。你認為你可以嗎？」

【註】 *drop off* 放置；擱下　　*dry clean* 乾洗
special (ˈspɛʃəl ) *adj.* 特別的
*pay attention to* 注意
vacation ( veˈkeʃən ) *n.* 假期
*go on vacation* 去度假　　*take care of* 照顧
favor (ˈfevɚ ) *n.* 幫忙　　*do sb. a favor* 幫助某人
watch ( watʃ ) *v.* 看顧　　*a couple of* 兩個；幾個

**A2**： I'd say, "I really need your help.  I'm going
out of town and there is no one to take care
of my dog.  Can you do it for me?"

我會說：「我真的需要你的幫忙。我將要出城，
但沒有人照顧我的狗。你可以幫我嗎？」

**A3**： I'd say, "I'll be gone for a few days next week.
I need to find someone to take care of my dog.
Can you help me out?"

我會說：「我下個禮拜將會出門幾天。我需要找
人照顧我的狗。你可以幫我嗎？」

【註】 town〔taʊn〕*n.* 城鎮；市中心
*go out of town* 出城；到鄉下
gone〔gɔn〕*adj.* 離開的　*a few* 一些
*next week* 下週　　find〔faɪnd〕*v.* 找到
*help sb. out* 幫助某人

＊請將下列自我介紹的句子再唸一遍，請開始：

My seat number is (複試座位號碼) , and my test number is
(初試准考證號碼).

# 初級英語檢定測驗第二階段

# 寫作口說能力測驗⑤

## 寫作能力測驗

本測驗共有兩部份。第一部份為單句寫作，第二部份為段落寫作。測驗時間為 40 分鐘。

### 第一部份：單句寫作

請將答案寫在答案紙上對應的題號旁，如有文法、用字、拼字、標點符號、大小寫等之錯誤，將予扣分。

### 第 1～5 題：句子改寫

請依題目之提示，將原句依指定型式改寫，並將改寫的句子完整地寫在答案紙上。

注意：須寫出提示之文字及標點符號。

例：題目：I am fine.

She ＿＿＿＿＿＿＿.

在答案紙上寫：***She is fine.***

1. The Lees are going camping this summer.

The Lees ＿＿＿＿＿＿＿＿＿＿＿＿＿＿ last summer.

2. We will be able to see the lake from the mountaintop.

Will ＿＿＿＿＿＿＿＿＿＿＿＿＿＿＿＿＿?

3. Nancy has a piano class today.

   Nancy _____ yesterday.

4. What will you do if you miss the train?

   If you _____?

5. Please take the red pencil to Mrs. Jones.

   Please take Mrs. Jones _____.

第 6～10 題：句子合併

   請依照題目指示，將兩句合併成一句。並將合併的句子完整地寫
   在答案紙上。

   注意：須寫出提示之文字及標點符號。

例：題目：John has a cap.

         The cap is purple.

         John _____ cap.

   在答案紙上寫：***John has a purple cap.***

6. Debbie will watch TV.

   Debbie will do her homework first.

   Debbie will _____ before she _____.

7. Did you remember to bring the file?

   The file was on my desk.

   Did _____?

8. Danny wanted to save money.

He found a part-time job.

Danny _____ because _____.

9. You saw a horror movie last night.

Did you enjoy it?

Did _____ that _____?

10. You will be late for your appointment.

You leave right now.

Unless you _____.

第 11～15 題：重組

請將題目中所有提示的字詞整合成一有意義的句子，並將重組的句子完整地寫在答案紙上。

注意：須寫出提示之文字及標點符號。（答案中必須使用所有提示的字詞，且不能隨意增減字詞，否則不予計分。）

例：題目：John _____.

this morning / late / was / again

在答案紙上寫：***John was late again this morning.***

11. We _____.

the movie / for / were / minutes / late / ten

12. My _____.

　　to school / than usual / me / to come / teacher / earlier / told

13. The _____.

　　was / man / young / package / a / delivered / by

14. We _____.

　　the ticket window / waited / opened / in line / until

15. Weren't _____?

　　the books / able to / in the library / you / find

## 第二部份：段落寫作

　　題目： 蘇珊（Susan）非常喜歡約翰（John），所以寫了一封
　　　　　情書給他，可是被拒絕了。請根據圖片內容寫一篇約
　　　　　50 字的簡短描述。

# 口說能力測驗

* 請在 15 秒內完成並唸出下列自我介紹的句子，請開始：

My seat number is （複試座位號碼）, and my test number is （初試准考證號碼）.

## I. 複誦

共五題。題目不印在試題上，由耳機播出，每題播出兩次，兩次之間大約有一到二秒的間隔。聽完兩次後，請馬上複誦一次。

## II. 朗讀句子與短文

共有五個句子及一篇短文，請先利用一分鐘的時間閱讀試題上的句子與短文，然後在一分鐘內以正常的速度，清楚正確的朗讀一遍。

One　: I had no idea that the test was today!

Two　: Rice is the main crop of this country.

Three : Did you say that you agree or disagree?

Four　: I'd like to buy a dozen roses.

Five　: The ferry leaves at 8:30 every day except Sunday.

Six : I had a terrible cold last week. I was coughing and my nose was running. I really felt terrible! Finally, I went to see a doctor. He told me to rest, and he gave some medicine. The medicine made me feel a little better, but it didn't cure my cold. But after a few days I got better anyway. Now I am feeling fine.

## III. 回答問題

共七題。題目不印在試題上,由耳機播出,每題播出兩次,兩次之間大約有一到二秒的間隔。聽完兩次後,請馬上回答,每題回答時間為 15 秒,請在作答時間內儘量的表達。

＊請將下列自我介紹的句子再唸一遍,請開始:

My seat number is (複試座位號碼) , and my test number is (初試准考證號碼).

# 寫作口說能力測驗 ⑤ 詳解

## 寫作能力測驗詳解

**第一部份：單句寫作**

第 1～5 題：句子改寫

1. The Lees are going camping this summer.
   The Lees ＿＿＿＿＿＿＿＿＿＿＿＿＿＿＿＿＿ last summer.

   　重點結構： 過去式動詞

   　解　答： <u>The Lees went camping last summer.</u>

   　句型分析： 主詞＋過去式動詞＋時間副詞

   　說　明： 看到時間副詞 last summer（去年夏天），知道動詞
   須改爲過去式，表示「過去時間的動作」，故 are
   going camping 須改成 went camping。

   　* camp〔kæmp〕v. 露營　　***go camping*** 去露營

2. We will be able to see the lake from the mountaintop.
   Will ＿＿＿＿＿＿＿＿＿＿＿＿＿＿＿＿＿＿＿?

   　重點結構： 未來式肯定句改爲疑問句

   　解　答： <u>Will we be able to see the lake from the
   mountaintop?</u>

   　句型分析： 助動詞＋主詞＋be able to＋動詞原形＋地方副詞？

   　說　明： 含有助動詞 will 的直述句改成疑問句，助動詞 will
   與主詞 we 要倒裝，並把句號改成問號。

   　* ***be able to V.*** 能夠　　lake〔lek〕n. 湖
   mountaintop〔'mauntn̩ˌtɑp〕n. 山頂

3. Nancy has a piano class today.

Nancy ＿＿＿＿＿＿＿＿＿＿＿＿＿＿＿＿＿＿＿ yesterday.

　　重點結構：過去式動詞

　　　解　答：Nancy had a piano class yesterday.

　　句型分析：主詞＋過去式動詞＋時間副詞

　　　說　明：看到時間副詞 yesterday（昨天）可知，動詞須改爲
　　　　　　　過去式，表示「過去時間的動作」，故 has 改成 had。

　　* piano〔pɪˋæno〕n. 鋼琴　　class〔klæs〕n. 課

4. What will you do if you miss the train?

If you ＿＿＿＿＿＿＿＿＿＿＿＿＿＿＿＿＿＿＿＿＿＿？

　　重點結構：if 的用法

　　　解　答：If you miss the train, what will you do?

　　句型分析：If＋主詞＋動詞＋,＋疑問詞＋助動詞＋主詞＋
　　　　　　　原形動詞？

　　　說　明：if 後面接條件子句，常放在主要子句之後，若 if 放
　　　　　　　在句首，則條件子句和主要子句之間須加一個逗號。

　　* miss〔mɪs〕v. 錯過　　train〔tren〕n. 火車

5. Please take the red pencil to Mrs. Jones.

Please take Mrs. Jones ＿＿＿＿＿＿＿＿＿＿＿＿＿＿＿＿＿．

　　重點結構：take 做授與動詞的用法

　　　解　答：Please take Mrs. Jones the red pencil.

　　句型分析：Please＋take＋直接受詞（人）＋間接受詞（物）

　　説　明：take ( 拿 ) 有兩種用法：
　　　　　　$\Big\{$ ① take + *sb.* + *sth.*
　　　　　　　　② take + *sth.* + to + *sb.*
　　　　　　本題的用法爲第一種。

　　* red〔rɛd〕*adj.* 紅色的　　pencil〔ˈpɛnsl〕*n.* 鉛筆


## 第 6～10 題：句子合併

6. Debbie will watch TV.

　Debbie will do her homework first.

　Debbie will ＿＿＿＿＿＿＿ before she ＿＿＿＿＿＿＿.

　　重點結構：before 的用法

　　解　答：<u>Debbie will do her homework before she</u>
　　　　　　<u>watches TV.</u>

　　句型分析：主詞 + 動詞 + before + 主詞 + 動詞

　　説　明：由副詞 first ( 先 ) 可知，黛比將會先做功課，再看
　　　　　　電視，用 before「在～之前」來表示事情的先後順
　　　　　　序，故 do her homework 放在 before 之前，watch
　　　　　　TV 放在 before 之後，而 before 所引導表「時間」
　　　　　　的副詞子句中，不可用未來式，要用現在式代替未
　　　　　　來式，主詞 Debbie 爲第三人稱單數，故 watch 要
　　　　　　加 es。

　　* homework〔ˈhom͵wɝk〕*n.* 家庭作業


7. Did you remember to bring the file?

　The file was on my desk.

　Did ＿＿＿＿＿＿＿＿＿＿＿＿＿＿＿＿＿＿＿＿＿＿?

　　重點結構：that 引導形容詞子句的用法

解　答：<u>Did you remember to bring the file (that/which</u> <u>was) on my desk?</u>

句型分析：Did + 主詞 + 動詞 + 不定詞 + ( that/which ) + 形容詞子句？

說　明：句意為「你記得帶我辦公桌上的那個檔案來嗎？」 在合併兩句時，用關係代名詞 that 或 which 代替 先行詞 the file，在形容詞子句中做主詞，引導形 容詞子句，又形容詞子句中的關代和 be 動詞可一 起省略，故 that/which was 可省略不寫。

\* remember〔rɪˋmɛmbɚ〕v. 記得　　bring〔brɪŋ〕v. 帶來 file〔faɪl〕n. 檔案　　desk〔dɛsk〕n. 辦公桌

8. Danny wanted to save money.

He found a part time job.

Danny ＿＿＿＿＿＿＿＿＿ because ＿＿＿＿＿＿＿＿＿＿＿.

重點結構：because 的用法

解　答：<u>Danny found a part-time job because he wanted</u> <u>to save money.</u>

句型分析：主詞 + 動詞 + because + 主詞 + 動詞

說　明：連接詞 because（因為）引導副詞子句，後面接原 因，故將結果 Danny found a part-time job 放在 because 之前，原因 he wanted to save money 放 在 because 之後。

\* save〔sev〕v. 存（錢）　　part-time〔ˋpɑrtˋtaɪm〕adj. 兼差的 job〔dʒɑb〕n. 工作

9. You saw a horror movie last night.

Did you enjoy it?

Did _____ that _____?

**重點結構：** that 引導形容詞子句的用法

　**解　答：** Did you enjoy the horror movie that you saw last night?

**句型分析：** 助動詞＋主詞＋動詞原形＋that＋主詞＋動詞＋時間副詞？

　**說　明：** that 在此為關係代名詞，代替先行詞 the horror movie，引導形容詞子句。本題的意思是「你喜歡你昨天晚上看的恐怖片嗎？」Did you enjoy it 為主要問句，但是 it 在此指的是「昨天晚上看的恐怖片」，故 it 要改成 the horror movie，後面接形容詞子句 that you saw last night。

\* horror (ˈhɑrɚ) *adj.* 恐怖的　　movie (ˈmuvɪ) *n.* 電影
*horror movie* 恐怖片　　enjoy ( ɪnˈdʒɔɪ ) *v.* 喜歡

10. You will be late for your appointment.

You leave right now.

Unless you _____.

**重點結構：** unless 的用法

　**解　答：** Unless you leave right now, you will be late for your appointment.

**句型分析：** Unless＋主詞＋動詞＋,＋主詞＋助動詞＋be 動詞原形＋形容詞片語

說　明：unless（除非）爲表條件的從屬連接詞，後面應接
條件子句，故先寫 Unless you leave right now，
再寫 you will be late for your appointment。在此
要注意的是，unless 放在句首時，條件子句和主要
子句之間須加一個逗點。

* late〔 let 〕 *adj.* 遲到的　　appointment〔 ə'pɔɪntmənt 〕 *n.* 約會
leave〔 liv 〕 *v.* 離開　　***right now*** 現在；立刻

## 第 11～15 題：重組

11. We _____.

the movie / for / were / minutes / late / ten

重點結構：「be late for + 受詞」的用法

解　答：<u>We were ten minutes late for the movie.</u>

句型分析：主詞 + be 動詞 + 時間副詞 + late for + 受詞

說　明：本句的意思是「我們看電影遲到了十分鐘」，句型
「be late for + 受詞」表示對這件事（受詞）來說
太遲了。ten minutes 爲時間副詞，用來強調遲到
了多久。

* minute〔'mɪnɪt 〕 *n.* 分鐘

12. My _____.

to school / than usual / me / to come / teacher / earlier / told

重點結構：tell 的用法

解　答：<u>My teacher told me to come to school earlier
than usual.</u>

句型分析：主詞 + 動詞 + 受詞 + to V. + 副詞比較級 +
than usual

　　説　明：「tell *sb.* to V.」的句型表示「告訴某人去做～」，
　　　　　　這題的意思是「我的老師告訴我，要比平常還早一
　　　　　　點到學校」，比平常還早，即 earlier than usual。

　　* early（'ɜlɪ）*adv.* 早　　***than usual*** 比平常

## 13. The _____.

was / man / young / package / a / delivered / by

　　重點結構：被動語態的用法

　　　解　答：The package was delivered by a young man.

　　句型分析：主詞 + be 動詞 + 過去分詞 + by + 受詞

　　　説　明：依句意，「包裹是被一個年輕男子送來的」，主詞
　　　　　　　The package 只能「被」遞送，被動語態的用法
　　　　　　　為「be 動詞 + 過去分詞」。

　　* package（'pækɪdʒ）*n.* 包裹　　deliver（dɪ'lɪvɚ）*v.* 遞送
　　young（jʌŋ）*adj.* 年輕的

## 14. We _____.

the ticket window / waited / opened / in line / until

　　重點結構：until 的用法

　　　解　答：We waited in line until the ticket window opened.

　　句型分析：主詞 + 動詞 + until + 主詞 + 動詞

　　　説　明：until（直到）為連接詞，引導表「時間」的副詞子
　　　　　　　句。句意為，「我們排隊直到售票口開始營業」。因
　　　　　　　此先寫主要子句 We waited in line，再寫副詞子句
　　　　　　　until the ticket window opened。

　　* wait（wet）*v.* 等待　　***wait in line*** 排隊等候
　　ticket（'tɪkɪt）*n.* 票；入場券　　window（'wɪndo）*n.* 窗戶
　　***ticket window*** 售票口　　open（'opən）*v.* 開始營業

15. Weren't _____?

   the books / able to / in the library / you / find

   > **重點結構：** be able to 問句
   >
   > **解　答：** <u>Weren't you able to find the books in the library?</u>
   >
   > **句型分析：** 過去式 be 動詞否定 + 主詞 + able to + 動詞
   > 　　　　　　 + 地方副詞？
   >
   > **說　明：** 含有 be able to 的疑問句，須將 be 動詞與主詞倒裝，
   > 　　　　　　 故先寫 Weren't you able to，而 to 後面要接原形動
   > 　　　　　　 詞，故再寫 find the books，in the library 為地方副
   > 　　　　　　 詞，放在句尾。
   >
   > \* **be able to V**. 能夠～　　find〔faɪnd〕v. 找到
   > 　 library〔'laɪ,brɛrɪ〕n. 圖書館

## 第二部份：段落寫作

【作文範例】

　　Susan liked John very much. So she wrote a love letter
to John. But John refused her letter. He did not like Susan
because she was not beautiful. Susan decided to change.
She went on a diet and she exercised every day. One year
later, Susan was very beautiful. Many boys wanted to be
her friend. When John saw Susan, he was very surprised.

> \* love〔lʌv〕n. 愛　　letter〔'lɛtə〕n. 信
> 　 **love letter** 情書　　refuse〔rɪ'fjuz〕v. 拒絕
> 　 decide〔dɪ'saɪd〕v. 決定　　change〔tʃendʒ〕v. 改變
> 　 **go on a diet** 開始節食　　exercise〔'ɛksə,saɪz〕v. 運動
> 　 later〔'letə〕adv. 之後　　surprised〔sə'praɪzd〕adj. 驚訝的

# 口說能力測驗詳解

\* 請在 15 秒內完成並唸出下列自我介紹的句子，請開始：

My seat number is （複試座位號碼）, and my test number is （初試准考證號碼）.

## I. 複誦

共五題。題目不印在試題上，由耳機播出，每題播出兩次，兩次之間大約有一到二秒的間隔。聽完兩次後，請馬上複誦一次。

1. This is a good restaurant. 這是一間很好的餐廳。

2. I'll call you later. 我待會會打給你。

3. Did you enjoy the show? 你喜歡那個表演嗎？

4. Please close the door. 請關門。

5. This is my favorite band. 這是我最喜歡的樂團。

【註】 restaurant（'rɛstərənt）*n.* 餐廳
call（kɔl）*v.* 打電話給　　later（'letɚ）*adv.* 待會
enjoy（ɪn'dʒɔɪ）*v.* 喜歡　　show（ʃo）*n.* 表演
close（kloz）*v.* 關　　door（dor）*n.* 門
favorite（'fevərɪt）*adj.* 最喜歡的
band（bænd）*n.* 樂團

## II. 朗讀句子與短文

共有五個句子及一篇短文，請先利用一分鐘的時間閱讀試題上的句子與短文，然後在一分鐘內以正常的速度，清楚正確的朗讀一遍。

One : I had no idea that the test was today!
我不知道是今天考試！

Two : Rice is the main crop of this country.
稻米是這個國家主要的農作物。

Three : Did you say that you agree or disagree?
你有說你同意或不同意嗎？

Four : I'd like to buy a dozen roses.
我想要買一打玫瑰。

Five : The ferry leaves at 8:30 every day except Sunday.
那艘渡輪每天八點半開船，除了星期天。

【註】 *have no idea* 不知道　　test〔tɛst〕*n.* 考試；測驗
rice〔raɪs〕*n.* 稻米　　main〔men〕*adj.* 主要的
crop〔krɑp〕*n.* 農作物　　country〔'kʌntrɪ〕*n.* 國家
agree〔ə'gri〕*v.* 同意　　disagree〔͵dɪsə'gri〕*v.* 不同意
*would like* 想要　　buy〔baɪ〕*v.* 買
dozen〔'dʌzn̩〕*n.* 一打；十二個　　rose〔roz〕*n.* 玫瑰
ferry〔'fɛrɪ〕*n.* 渡輪　　leave〔liv〕*v.* 離開；啟程
except〔ɪk'sɛpt〕*prep.* 除了…之外
Sunday〔'sʌnde〕*n.* 星期天

Six : I had a terrible cold last week.  I was coughing
and my nose was running.  I really felt terrible!
Finally, I went to see a doctor.  He told me to
rest, and he gave me some medicine.  The
medicine made me feel a little better, but it
didn't cure my cold.  But after a few days I got
better anyway.  Now I am feeling fine.

上個禮拜，我得了重感冒。我咳嗽，而且還流鼻水。
我真的覺得很糟糕！最後，我去看了醫生。他告訴我
要休息，然後給了我一些藥。那些藥讓我感覺好了一
點，但是並沒有完全治好我的感冒。不過幾天之後，
我還是好了。現在我感覺很好。

【註】 terrible (ˈtɛrəbl̩ ) adj. 嚴重的；糟糕的
　　　cold ( kold ) n. 感冒　　　*last week* 上週
　　　cough ( kɔf ) v. 咳嗽　　　nose ( noz ) n. 鼻子
　　　running (ˈrʌnɪŋ ) adj. 流鼻水的
　　　really (ˈriəlɪ ) adv. 真地　　　feel ( fil ) v. 覺得
　　　finally (ˈfaɪnlɪ ) adv. 最後；終於
　　　rest ( rɛst ) v. 休息　　　medicine (ˈmɛdəsn̩ ) n. 藥
　　　*a little* 一點　　　better (ˈbɛtɚ ) adj. 較好的
　　　cure ( kjur ) v. 治療；治好　　　*a few* 一些；幾個
　　　anyway (ˈɛnɪˌwe ) adv. 不管怎樣；還是
　　　fine ( faɪn ) adj. 很好的

## Ⅲ. 回答問題

共七題。題目不印在試題上，由耳機播出，每題播出兩次，兩次之間大約有一到二秒的間隔。聽完兩次後，請馬上回答，每題回答時間爲 15 秒，請在作答時間內儘量的表達。

**1. Q** : Today is your friend's birthday.  You have a gift for him or her.  What do you say to your friend?

今天是你朋友的生日。你有一個禮物要給他（她）。你會對你的朋友說什麼？

**A1** : I'd say, "Happy birthday!  This is for you.  I hope you like it."

我會說：「生日快樂！這是給你的。希望你會喜歡。」

**A2** : I'd say, "I heard today is your birthday.  Here is a little present for you.  It's nothing extravagant, but I hope you enjoy it."

我會說：「我聽說今天是你的生日。這裡有一個小禮物要給你。不是什麼很貴的東西，但我希望你會喜歡。」

【註】 birthday〔'bɝθ,de〕*n.* 生日
　　　 gift〔gɪft〕*n.* 禮物　　　 hope〔hop〕*v.* 希望
　　　 hear〔hɪr〕*v.* 聽說　　　 little〔'lɪtḷ〕*adj.* 小的
　　　 present〔'prɛzn̩t〕*n.* 禮物（= *gift*）
　　　 extravagant〔ɪk'strævəgənt〕*adj.* 奢侈的
　　　 enjoy〔ɪn'dʒɔɪ〕*v.* 喜歡

**A3**：I'd say, "Happy birthday!  I wish you all the best.
Here is a little something to celebrate the day."
我會說：「生日快樂！我祝你心想事成。這裡有個小東
西用來祝賀你的生日。」

---

**2. Q**　：You get on a bus and the only seat available is on
the aisle.  You want to sit next to the window
because you often feel sick on buses.  What do
you say to the person in the window seat?
你上了公車，唯一的空位是靠走道的位子。你想要坐在
窗邊，因為你常常在公車上感到不舒服。你會對坐在靠
窗的位子上的人說什麼？

**A1**：I'd say, "Excuse me.  Would you mind switching
seats with me?  I get a little dizzy on buses."
我會說：「不好意思。你介意和我換位子嗎？我在公車
上會覺得有點頭暈。」

【註】　wish〔wɪʃ〕v. 希望　　*all the best* 祝心想事成
celebrate〔'sɛlə,bret〕v. 慶祝　　*get on* 上（車）
*the only* 唯一的　　seat〔sit〕n. 座位
available〔ə'veləbḷ〕adj. 可獲得的；有空位的
aisle〔aɪl〕n. 走道　　*next to* 在…隔壁
often〔'ɔfən〕adv. 常常　　sick〔sɪk〕adj. 不舒服的
person〔'pɜsṇ〕n. 人　　mind〔maɪnd〕v. 介意
switch〔swɪtʃ〕v. 交換　　*a little* 有點
dizzy〔'dɪzɪ〕adj. 頭暈的

**A2**：I'd say, "Hi.  I really need to sit next to a window.  Would you mind very much sitting in the aisle seat?"

我會說：「嗨。我真的需要坐在窗戶旁邊。你會非常介意坐靠走道的位子嗎？」

**A3**：I'd say, "Could I ask you a favor?  I need to sit by a window or I may get sick.  Do you think we could trade places?"

我會說：「可以請你幫個忙嗎？我需要坐在窗戶旁邊，不然我可能會感到不舒服。你覺得我們可以交換一下位子嗎？」

---

**3. Q**：Imagine you are at a café waiting for a friend.  He or she is 20 minutes late.  What would you do?

想像一下你正在咖啡廳裡等一位朋友。他（她）遲到了二十分鐘。你會做什麼？

【註】 hi〔haɪ〕interj. 嗨　　need〔nid〕v. 需要
favor〔'fevɚ〕n. 幫忙　　**ask sb. a favor** 請某人幫忙
**sit by** 坐在…的旁邊　　or〔ɔr〕conj. 否則；不然
trade〔tred〕v. 交換　　place〔ples〕n. 座位
imagine〔ɪ'mædʒɪn〕v. 想像　　café〔kæ'fe〕n. 咖啡廳
**wait for** 等待　　late〔let〕adj. 遲到的

**A1**：I would simply call her.　I would ask her if she is OK, or if she forgot our appointment.　I wouldn't get mad until I knew the reason.

我會打電話給她。我會問她還好嗎，或是她忘了我們的約會。在我知道原因之前我不會生氣。

**A2**：I'd probably wait a little longer.　Traffic can be bad sometimes.　It often makes people late.

我可能會再等久一點。有時候交通情況可能很糟。常會讓人遲到。

**A3**：I'd call him, of course.　I'd find out what the problem is.　I'd say, "I'm waiting at the café. Where are you?"

我當然會打電話給他。我會找出是什麼問題。我會說：「我在咖啡廳裡等你。你在哪裡？」

【註】　simply〔'sɪmplɪ〕*adv.* 單單地；只
　　ask〔æsk〕*v.* 問　　OK〔'o'ke〕*adj.* 好的；沒問題的
　　forget〔fə'gɛt〕*v.* 忘記
　　appointment〔ə'pɔɪntmənt〕*n.* 約會
　　*not…until~* 直到~才…　　mad〔mæd〕*adj.* 生氣的
　　reason〔'rizn̩〕*n.* 原因；理由
　　probably〔'prɑbəblɪ〕*adv.* 可能
　　long〔lɔŋ〕*adj.* 時間久的
　　traffic〔'træfɪk〕*n.* 交通　　bad〔bæd〕*adj.* 糟糕的
　　sometimes〔'sʌm,taɪmz〕*adv.* 有時候
　　make〔mek〕*v.* 使　　*of course* 當然
　　*find out* 查出；找出　　problem〔'prɑbləm〕*n.* 問題

**4. Q** ： You buy a toaster at a department store.  When you get home you find out that it doesn't work, so you take it back to the store.  What do you say to the salesclerk?　你在百貨公司裡買了一台烤麵包機。當你回家的時候，你發現烤麵包機故障了，所以你把它帶回店裡。你會對店員說什麼？

**A1**： I'd say, "I just bought this toaster.  But it doesn't work.  Can I exchange it for another one?"　我會說：「我剛買這台烤麵包機。但是它故障了。我可以換一台嗎？」

**A2**： I'd say, "Hi.  I bought this toaster here.  There's something wrong with it.  I'd like to get my money back."　我會說：「嗨。我在這裡買了這台烤麵包機。它有點問題。我想退錢。」

**A3**： I'd say, "Excuse me.  I want to return this toaster.  It doesn't work."　我會說：「抱歉。我想要退還這台烤麵包機。它故障了。」

【註】 toaster ('tostə ) *n.* 烤麵包機
　　　***department store*** 百貨公司　　***get home*** 回家
　　　***find out*** 發現　　work ( wɜk ) *v.* 運作
　　　***take*** *sth.* ***back to*** 帶著某物回到…
　　　store ( stor ) *n.* 商店　　salesclerk ('selz͵klɜk ) *n.* 店員
　　　just ( dʒʌst ) *adv.* 剛剛　　exchange ( ɪks'tʃendʒ ) *v.* 交換
　　　another ( ə'nʌðə ) *adj.* 另一的
　　　***There's something wrong with*～** ～有問題
　　　***get back*** 拿回　　return ( rɪ'tɜn ) *v.* 退還

**5. Q** : You are visiting the zoo with your friends.  You
want to take a picture with all of them.  Ask a
stranger to help you take the picture.

你和朋友到動物園參觀。你想和他們一起照一張相。
請一個陌生人幫你們拍照。

**A1** : "Hi.  Sorry to bother you.  Could you take a
picture of me and my friends?"

「嗨。很抱歉打擾你。你可以幫我和我的朋友拍一
張照片嗎？」

**A2** : "Excuse me.  Would you mind taking a picture
of us?  Just push this button.  Thanks a lot!"

「對不起。你介意幫我們拍一張照片嗎？只要按下
這個按鈕就好。非常謝謝你！」

**A3** : "Hi, there.  Could I ask you a favor?  Could
you take a picture of us with this camera?"

「嗨，你好。可以請你幫我一個忙嗎？你可以用這
台相機幫我們拍張照嗎？」

【註】　visit ('vɪzɪt ) v. 參觀　　zoo ( zu ) n. 動物園
*take a picture* 拍照　　ask ( æsk ) v. 請求
stranger ('strendʒɚ ) n. 陌生人
help ( hɛlp ) v. 幫忙　　bother ('baðɚ ) v. 打擾
push ( puʃ ) v. 按；推　　button ('bʌtn̩ ) n. 按鈕
*Hi, there.* 嗨，你好。　　*Thanks a lot.* 非常謝謝你。
camera ('kæmərə ) n. 相機

**6. Q** ： You want to reserve a hotel room for the weekend. What do you say to the person who answers the phone?

你想為週末訂一間旅館的房間。你會跟接電話的人說什麼？

**A1** ： "Hello. I'd like to make a reservation. I need a room for Friday and Saturday night. The name is Smith."

「哈囉。我想訂房。我需要一個房間，星期五和星期六晚上。名字是史密斯。」

**A2** ： "Good morning. Do you have any rooms available this weekend? Could you tell me the price? Thank you."

「早安。你們這個週末還有空房間嗎？你可以告訴我價格嗎？謝謝你。」

【註】 reserve〔rɪˈzɝv〕v. 預訂

　　　hotel〔hoˈtɛl〕n. 旅館　　room〔rum〕n. 房間

　　　weekend〔ˈwikˌɛnd〕n. 週末

　　　answer〔ˈænsɚ〕v. 接（電話）

　　　phone〔fon〕n. 電話　　hello〔həˈlo〕interj. 哈囉

　　　reservation〔ˌrɛzɚˈveʃən〕n. 預訂

　　　name〔nem〕n. 名字　　Smith〔smɪθ〕n. 史密斯

　　　available〔əˈveləbḷ〕adj. 可獲得的；有空房的

　　　tell〔tɛl〕v. 告訴　　price〔praɪs〕n. 價格

A3："Hi. I'm calling to make a reservation. I need one room for this weekend. Are there any available?"

「嗨。我打電話來訂房。這個週末我需要一間房間。還有任何的空房嗎？」

7. Q ： You are getting ready to go to school. You cannot find one of the books you need. What do you do?

你已準備好要去上學了。你找不到其中一本你需要的書。你會怎麼做？

A1： First, I would calm down. Then I would look in my book bag and in my room again. If I still couldn't find it, I would ask my family for help.

首先，我會先鎮定下來。然後我會再看一次我的書包和房間。如果還是找不到，我就會請我的家人幫忙。

【註】 ready〔'rɛdɪ〕adj. 準備好的
**get ready to V.** 準備好要⋯
first〔fɜst〕adv. 首先　　calm〔kɑm〕v. 鎮定
**calm down** 鎮定下來　　**look in** 往⋯裡面看
**book bag** 書包　　again〔ə'gɛn〕adv. 再
still〔stɪl〕adv. 仍然　　family〔'fæməlɪ〕n. 家人
**ask sb. for help** 請某人幫忙

**A2**：I'd ask my brother. He often moves my things.
Chances are he took it.

我會問我弟弟。他常常動我的東西。有可能是他拿
走了。

**A3**：I'd ask my family if they had seen it. If no
one could find it, then I would go to school
without it. I'd ask a friend to share her book
with me.

我會問我的家人有沒有看到。如果沒有人找得到,
那我就會不帶那本書直接去學校了。我會請我的朋
友讓我和她看同一本書。

【註】 move〔muv〕*v.* 移動　　thing〔θɪŋ〕*n.* 東西
chance〔tʃæns〕*n.* 機會
(*The*) *chances are* (*that*)… 很可能;或許
if〔ɪf〕*conj.* 是否
without〔wɪð'aʊt〕*prep.* 沒有
share〔ʃɛr〕*v.* 分享;共用

＊請將下列自我介紹的句子再唸一遍,請開始:

My seat number is (複試座位號碼) , and my test number is
(初試准考證號碼) .

# 初級英語檢定測驗第二階段

# 寫作口説能力測驗⑥

## 寫作能力測驗

本測驗共有兩部份。第一部份為單句寫作，第二部份為段落寫作。測驗時間為 40 分鐘。

**第一部份：單句寫作**

請將答案寫在答案紙上對應的題號旁，如有文法、用字、拼字、標點符號、大小寫等之錯誤，將予扣分。

第 1～5 題：句子改寫

請依題目之提示，將原句依指定型式改寫，並將改寫的句子<u>完整</u>地寫在答案紙上。

注意：須寫出提示之文字及標點符號。

例：　題目：I am fine.

　　　She _____.

　　　在答案紙上寫：***She is fine.***

1. What is your nationality?

　Can you tell me _____?

2. I used to play ping-pong when I was in junior high school.

　I _____ yesterday.

3. I would go with you if I didn't have to study.

   I will _____.

4. This strawberry pie was made by Lydia.

   Was _____?

5. This is Donna's book, isn't it?

   This isn't _____ it?

第 6～10 題：句子合併

　　請依照題目指示，將兩句合併成一句。並將合併的句子<u>完整</u>地寫在答案紙上。

　　注意：須寫出提示之文字及標點符號。

例：　題目：John has a cap.

　　　　　　The cap is purple.

　　　　　　John _____ cap.

　　在答案紙上寫：***John has a purple cap.***

6. I don't want any coffee.

   I don't want any tea.

   I want neither _____.

7. You will go to the mall.

   I will go with you.

   I will _____ you.

8. You should take a rest.

    You will feel sleepy.

    You _____ or _____.

9. I have three sisters.

    I have one brother.

    I _____.

10. We can't see the movie.

    There are no more tickets.

    If _____.

第 11～15 題：重組

　　請將題目中所有提示的字詞整合成一有意義的句子，並將重組的
　　句子完整地寫在答案紙上。

　　注意：須寫出提示之文字及標點符號。( 答案中必須使用所有提
　　　　　示的字詞，且不能隨意增減字詞，否則不予計分。)

例： 題目： John _____.

　　　 this morning / late / was / again

　　在答案紙上寫：***John was late again this morning.***

11. This is _____.

    birthday / my / got / I / the bicycle / for / that

12. There _____.

time / to eat / no / is / lunch / us / for

13. Would _____?

consider / your hair / ever / having / you / dyed

14. Can _____?

the mall / me / how to / you / get to / tell

15. I _____.

this gift / Japan / from / brought / back

## 第二部份：段落寫作

題目：現在是聖誕節前夕。馬克（Mark）有二張電影票想找
人一起去看，沒想到大家都拒絕他。請根據圖片內容
寫一篇約 50 字的簡短描述。

# 口說能力測驗

\* 請在 15 秒內完成並唸出下列自我介紹的句子，請開始：

My seat number is (複試座位號碼), and my test number is (初試准考證號碼).

## I. 複誦

共五題。題目不印在試題上，由耳機播出，每題播出兩次，兩次之間大約有一到二秒的間隔。聽完兩次後，請馬上複誦一次。

## II. 朗讀句子與短文

共有五個句子及一篇短文，請先利用一分鐘的時間閱讀試題上的句子與短文，然後在一分鐘內以正常的速度，清楚正確的朗讀一遍。

One : There is a bookstore right around the corner.

Two : This is the best apple pie I've ever had.

Three : I wish you all the best on your birthday.

Four : I used to live in a small town in the mountains.

Five : I'm playing golf with Jim on Saturday.

Six ： I went window-shopping last weekend.　To my surprise, there was a big sale at the department store.　I found a jacket that I really liked, but I hadn't brought enough money with me. Fortunately, the store accepted credit cards.　I charged the jacket and the salesperson put it in a bag for me.　I was so happy to walk out of the store with my bargain.

## Ⅲ. 回答問題

共七題。題目不印在試題上，由耳機播出，每題播出兩次，兩次之間大約有一到二秒的間隔。聽完兩次後，請馬上回答，每題回答時間為 15 秒，請在作答時間內儘量的表達。

＊ 請將下列自我介紹的句子再唸一遍，請開始：

My seat number is （複試座位號碼）, and my test number is （初試准考證號碼）.

# 寫作口說能力測驗 ⑥ 詳解

## 寫作能力測驗詳解

### 第一部份：單句寫作

第 1～5 題：句子改寫

1. What is your nationality?
   Can you tell me ＿＿＿＿＿＿＿＿＿＿＿＿＿＿＿＿＿＿＿＿＿?

   > **重點結構：**直接問句改爲間接問句
   >
   > **解　答：**Can you tell me what your nationality is?
   >
   > **句型分析：**Can you tell me ＋ what ＋ 主詞 ＋ be 動詞？
   >
   > **說　明：**Can you tell me 後面須接受詞，故直接問句 What is your nationality 須改爲間接問句當受詞用，即「疑問詞＋主詞＋動詞」的形式。
   >
   > \* nationality〔͵næʃənˈælətɪ〕n. 國籍

2. I used to play ping-pong when I was in junior high school.
   I ＿＿＿＿＿＿＿＿＿＿＿＿＿＿＿＿＿＿＿ yesterday.

   > **重點結構：**過去式動詞
   >
   > **解　答：**I played ping-pong yesterday.
   >
   > **句型分析：**主詞＋過去式動詞＋時間副詞
   >
   > **說　明：**看到時間副詞 yesterday（昨天），知道動詞須改爲過去式，表示「過去時間的動作」，故 used to play 改成 played。
   >
   > \* **used to** 以前　　ping-pong〔ˈpɪŋ͵pɑŋ〕n. 乒乓球
   > **junior high school** 國中

3. I would go with you if I didn't have to study.
   I will _____.

   重點結構：假設語氣改成直說法

   解　答：<u>I will go with you if I don't have to study.</u>

   句型分析：主詞＋未來式助動詞＋原形動詞＋ if ＋主詞＋
   　　　　　現在式助動詞否定＋動詞原形

   說　明：題目原本是與現在事實相反的假設語氣，現在依提
   　　　　　示 will，可知要改為未來式的直說法，但是表「條
   　　　　　件」的副詞子句不能用未來式，要用現在代替未來，
   　　　　　故 didn't 改為 don't。

4. This strawberry pie was made by Lydia.
   Was _____?

   重點結構：直述句改為疑問句

   解　答：<u>Was this strawberry pie made by Lydia?</u>

   句型分析：be 動詞＋主詞＋動詞？

   說　明：直述句改成疑問句時，須將 be 動詞與主詞倒裝，
   　　　　　並把句號改成問號。

   * strawberry (ˈstrɔˌbɛrɪ ) n. 草莓　　**strawberry pie** 草莓派

5. This is Donna's book, isn't it?
   This isn't _____ it?

   重點結構：附加問句的用法

   解　答：<u>This isn't Donna's book, is it?</u>

   句型分析：主詞＋ be 動詞否定的縮寫＋, ＋ be 動詞（肯定）＋
   　　　　　代名詞？

說　明：當敘述句的 be 動詞爲否定，則附加問句中的 be 動
　　　　詞應用肯定，反之，當敘述句的 be 動詞爲肯定，
　　　　則附加問句中的 be 動詞應用否定，這題的意思是
　　　　「這不是唐娜的書，是嗎？」

第 6～10 題：句子合併

6. I don't want any coffee.
   I don't want any tea.
   I want neither ＿＿＿＿＿＿＿＿＿＿＿＿＿＿＿＿＿＿＿＿＿＿.

　　重點結構：「neither…nor～」的用法

　　解　答：<u>I want neither coffee nor tea.</u>

　　句型分析：主詞＋動詞＋neither＋A＋nor＋B

　　說　明：「neither…nor～」爲對等連接詞，用來連接文法
　　　　　　作用相同的單字、片語或子句，本身已有否定的意
　　　　　　思，故用在肯定的句型中，本題連接兩個名詞，即
　　　　　　coffee 和 tea，句意爲，「我不想喝咖啡，也不想喝
　　　　　　茶」。

7. You will go to the mall.
   I will go with you.
   I will ＿＿＿＿＿＿＿＿＿＿＿＿＿＿＿＿＿＿＿＿＿＿ you.

　　重點結構：句子基本結構

　　解　答：<u>I will go to the mall with you</u>

　　句型分析：主詞＋動詞＋with＋受詞

　　說　明：句意爲「我會和你一起去購物中心」，with 表示
　　　　　　「和…一起」的意思。

　　＊ mall〔mɔl〕*n.* 購物中心（＝ *shopping center*）

8. You should take a rest.
   You will feel sleepy.
   You ＿＿＿＿＿＿＿＿＿＿＿ or ＿＿＿＿＿＿＿＿＿＿＿.

　　重點結構：or（否則）的用法

　　　解　答：You should take a rest or you will feel sleepy.

　　句型分析：主詞＋助動詞＋動詞＋or＋主詞＋助動詞＋動詞

　　　説　明：or 作「否則」解時，前面常會放含有「命令、勸告」
　　　　　　　的句子，表示受話者若不接受該命令或勸告，可能
　　　　　　　產生的結果就是 or 之後的句子。依題意「你應該休
　　　　　　　息一下，否則你會很想睡覺」，所以將第一句放在
　　　　　　　or 之前，第二句放在 or 之後即可。

　　* take a rest 休息一下　　　sleepy〔'slipɪ〕adj. 想睡的

9. I have three sisters.
   I have one brother.
   I ＿＿＿＿＿＿＿＿＿＿＿＿＿＿＿＿＿＿＿.

　　重點結構：and 的用法

　　　解　答：I have three sisters and one brother.

　　句型分析：主詞＋動詞＋A＋and＋B

　　　説　明：連接詞 and（和）爲對等連接詞，連接前後文法功
　　　　　　　能相同的單字、片語或句子，此題的 and 連接二個
　　　　　　　名詞，即 three sisters 和 one brother。

10. We can't see the movie.
    There are no more tickets.
    If ＿＿＿＿＿＿＿＿＿＿＿＿＿＿＿＿＿＿＿.

　　重點結構：if 的用法

解　答：<u>If there are no more tickets, we can't see the movie.</u>

句型分析：If + there are + 名詞 + , + 主詞 + 助動詞否定 + 原形動詞

說　明：本題的意思是「如果沒有票，我們就無法看電影」，if ( 如果 ) 後面應接條件子句，故先寫 there are no more tickets，再寫主要子句 we can't see the movie。要注意的是，當 if 放在句首時，條件子句和主要子句之間須加一個逗號。

\* movie ('muvɪ ) *n.* 電影　　　ticket ('tɪkɪt ) *n.* 電影票

第 11~15 題：重組

11. This is ＿＿＿＿＿＿＿＿＿＿＿＿＿＿＿＿＿＿＿＿＿.
    birthday / my / got / I / the bicycle / for / that

重點結構：that 引導形容詞子句的用法

解　答：<u>This is the bicycle that I got for my birthday.</u>

句型分析：This + be 動詞 + 主詞補語 + that + 形容詞子句

說　明：that 在這裡當關係代名詞，引導形容詞子句，即「關代 + 主詞 + 動詞」，修飾主詞補語，故 This is 後面接主詞補語 the bicycle，再寫 that 子句。本句的意思為「這就是我為我生日買的腳踏車」。

12. There ＿＿＿＿＿＿＿＿＿＿＿＿＿＿＿＿＿＿＿＿＿.
    time / to eat / no / is / lunch / us / for

重點結構：「there is no + 名詞」的用法

解　答：<u>There is no time for us to eat lunch.</u>

句型分析：There + be 動詞 + no + 名詞 + 介系詞 + 受詞 + to V.

説　明：表達「沒有」，除了可用「there＋be 動詞否定＋名
　　　　詞」，亦可用「there＋be 動詞＋no＋名詞」的形式，
　　　　be 動詞的單複數，須依其後的名詞（主詞）來決定。
　　　　本句的意思是「我們沒有時間吃午餐」。

13. Would _____?

consider / your hair / ever / having / you / dyed

　　重點結構：句子基本架構

　　解　答：<u>Would you ever consider having your hair dyed?</u>

　　句型分析：助動詞＋主詞＋副詞＋consider＋受詞？

　　説　明：本題的意思是，「你有考慮過要染頭髮嗎？」Would
　　　　　　後面接主詞 you，再找出動詞 consider，後面接受
　　　　　　詞 having your hair dyed；副詞 ever 用來修飾動
　　　　　　詞，放在 consider 之前。

　　* consider〔kən'sɪdə〕v. 考慮　　dye〔daɪ〕v. 染

14. Can _____?

the mall / me / how to / you / get to / tell

　　重點結構：間接問句的用法

　　解　答：<u>Can you tell me how to get to the mall?</u>

　　句型分析：Can you tell me＋how＋不定詞？

　　説　明：題目由助動詞 Can 開頭，而提示中有疑問詞 how，
　　　　　　可得知本題是考間接問句的用法，由疑問詞 how 所
　　　　　　引導的名詞子句，即「疑問詞＋不定詞」的形式，
　　　　　　作為 Can you tell me 的受詞，句意為「你可以告
　　　　　　訴我如何去購物中心嗎？」

　　* *get to* 到達　　mall〔mɔl〕n. 購物中心

15. I _____.

   this gift / Japan / from / brought / back

   　重點結構：句子基本架構

   　解　　答：I brought this gift back from Japan.

   　句型分析：主詞 + 動詞 + 地方副詞

   　說　　明：這題的意思是「我從日本帶回這個禮物」，主詞 I 後
   　　　　　　面應接動詞 brought this gift back，再接地方副詞
   　　　　　　from Japan。

   　* *bring sth. back* 帶回某物　　gift ( gɪft ) *n.* 禮物
   　　Japan ( dʒə'pæn ) *n.* 日本

## 第二部份：段落寫作

### 【作文範例】

　　It was *Christmas Eve*. Mark had two tickets to a new movie. He called his friend Cindy, but Cindy did not want to see the movie. Then Mark called May, but May said no. Wendy, Lisa, and Rachel also said no. Mark was confused. Why didn't anyone want to see the movie? Later that night, Mark saw all of his friends. They were standing in a line. They were waiting for Jay Chou to sign their CDs.

　* *Christmas Eve* 聖誕夜　　ticket ('tɪkɪt ) *n.* 票
   call ( kɔl ) *v.* 打電話給　　confused ( kən'fjuzd ) *adj.* 困惑的
   *later that night* 那天晚上較晚的時候　　*stand in line* 排隊
   *wait for* 等待　　sign ( saɪn ) *v.* 在…簽名
   *CD n.* 雷射唱片 ( = *compact disk* )

# 口說能力測驗詳解

\* 請在 15 秒內完成並唸出下列自我介紹的句子，請開始：

My seat number is （複試座位號碼），and my test number is （初試准考證號碼）.

## I. 複誦

共五題。題目不印在試題上，由耳機播出，每題播出兩次，兩次之間大約有一到二秒的間隔。聽完兩次後，請馬上複誦一次。

1. My sister's name is Sally. 我妹妹的名字是莎莉。

2. The watch is made of gold. 這只手錶是黃金做的。

3. I missed the bus this morning.
   今天早上我沒趕上公車。

4. The store is having a sale. 這家店正在舉行大拍賣。

5. Here is your order. 這是您的餐點。

【註】 name〔nem〕n. 名字　　Sally〔'sælɪ〕n. 莎莉
watch〔wɑtʃ〕n. 手錶　　*be made of* 由～製成
gold〔gold〕n. 黃金　　miss〔mɪs〕v. 錯過；未趕上
store〔stor〕n. 商店　　sale〔sel〕n. 拍賣
order〔'ɔrdɚ〕n. 餐點

## II. 朗讀句子與短文

　　共有五個句子及一篇短文，請先利用一分鐘的時間閱讀試題上
的句子與短文，然後在一分鐘內以正常的速度，清楚正確的朗
讀一遍。

One　　: There is a bookstore right around the corner.
　　　　　有一間書店就在轉角。

Two　　: This is the best apple pie I've ever had.
　　　　　這是我吃過最好吃的蘋果派。

Three : I wish you all the best on your birthday.
　　　　　我祝福你在生日當天一切順心。

Four　 : I used to live in a small town in the mountains.
　　　　　我以前住在山中的一個小城裡。

Five　 : I'm playing golf with Jim on Saturday.
　　　　　我星期六要和吉姆一起打高爾夫球。

【註】　bookstore ('buk͵stor ) n. 書店　　　right ( raɪt ) adv. 正好
　　　　corner ('kɔrnɚ ) n. 轉角　　*around the corner* 在轉角
　　　　best ( bɛst ) adj. 最好的　　*apple pie* 蘋果派
　　　　ever ('ɛvɚ ) adv. 曾經　　have ( hæv ) v. 吃
　　　　wish ( wɪʃ ) v. 希望；祝　　*all the best* 祝一切順心
　　　　birthday ('bɝθ͵de ) n. 生日　　*used to* 以前
　　　　live ( lɪv ) v. 住　　small ( smɔl ) adj. 小的
　　　　town ( taun ) n. 城鎮　　mountain ('mauntn̩ ) n. 山
　　　　play ( ple ) v. 打 ( 球 )　　golf ( gɑlf ) n. 高爾夫球
　　　　Jim ( dʒɪm ) n. 吉姆　　Saturday ('sætɚde ) n. 星期六

Six : I went window-shopping last weekend. To my surprise, there was a big sale at the department store. I found a jacket that I really liked, but I hadn't brought enough money with me. Fortunately, the store accepted credit cards. I charged the jacket and the salesperson put it in a bag for me. I was so happy to walk out of the store with my bargain.

上個週末，我去逛街瀏覽商店櫥窗。令我驚訝的是，百貨公司舉行大拍賣。我發現一件我很喜歡的夾克，但我沒帶足夠的錢。幸運的是，那家店接受信用卡。我刷卡買了那件夾克，然後店員就幫我把它放到袋子裡。我很高興地帶著我的特價品走出那家店。

【註】 *go window-shopping* 去逛街瀏覽商店櫥窗
weekend ('wik'ɛnd ) *n.* 週末　　*last weekend* 上週末
surprise ( sə'praɪz ) *n.* 驚訝
*to one's surprise* 讓某人驚訝的是
*department store* 百貨公司　　find ( faɪnd ) *v.* 發現
jacket ('dʒækɪt ) *n.* 夾克　　really ('riəlɪ ) *adv.* 真地
bring ( brɪŋ ) *v.* 帶　　enough ( ə'nʌf ) *adj.* 足夠的
fortunately ('fɔrtʃənɪtlɪ ) *adv.* 幸運地
accept ( ək'sɛpt ) *v.* 接受　　*credit card* 信用卡
charge ( tʃɑrdʒ ) *v.* 刷卡購買
salesperson ('selz,pɜsn̩ ) *n.* 店員
*put sth. in* 把某物放進…　　bag ( bæg ) *n.* 袋子
*walk out of* 從…走出去　　bargain ('bɑrgɪn ) *n.* 特價品

## III. 回答問題

共七題。題目不印在試題上，由耳機播出，每題播出兩次，兩次之間大約有一到二秒的間隔。聽完兩次後，請馬上回答，每題回答時間為 15 秒，請在作答時間內儘量的表達。

**1. Q** ： You overslept and missed your bus to school. If you wait for the next one, you will be late. Ask your mother to drive you to school.

你睡過頭，而且錯過了去學校的公車。如果等下一班，你就會遲到。請求你的媽媽開車載你去學校。

**A1** ： "Mom, I'm really sorry. I missed the bus and now I'm late for school. Could you take me this morning? I promise I won't do it again."

「媽，我真的很抱歉。我沒趕上公車，現在我上學要遲到了。今天早上妳可以帶我去嗎？我保證我不會再這樣了。」

**A2** ： "Mom, I really need your help. I missed my bus and I have a test this morning. Can you drive me to school?" 「媽，我真的很需要妳的幫忙。我沒趕上公車，而且今天早上我要考試。妳可以開車載我去學校嗎？」

【註】 oversleep〔'ovɚ'slip〕v. 睡過頭　　miss〔mɪs〕v. 錯過
*wait for* 等待　　next〔nɛkst〕adj. 下一個的
late〔let〕adj. 遲到的　　ask〔æsk〕v. 請求
drive〔draɪv〕v. 開車載（人）　　mom〔mɑm〕n. 媽
take〔tek〕v. 用（交通工具）載（人）
promise〔'prɑmɪs〕v. 保證　　again〔ə'gɛn〕adv. 再一次
help〔hɛlp〕n. 幫忙　　test〔tɛst〕n. 測驗；考試

**A3**："Mom, could you drive me to school today? If you don't, I'll be late and my teacher will punish me." 「媽，妳今天可以開車載我去學校嗎？如果妳不載我去的話，我會遲到，而且我的老師會處罰我。」

---

**2. Q** ：Your parents ask you to help with the housework, but you have to study for an exam. What do you say to them? 你的父母要求你幫忙做家事，但是你必須為了準備考試而唸書。你會對他們說什麼？

**A1**：I'd say, "I'm sorry. I have a lot of studying to do. There's a big test tomorrow."
我會說：「對不起。我有很多書要唸。明天有一個重要的考試。」

**A2**：I'd say, "I can help you, but I really should be studying. I have an important exam tomorrow."
我會說：「我可以幫忙，但是我真的應該讀書。我明天有一個很重要的考試。」

【註】 punish〔ˋpʌnɪʃ〕v. 處罰　　parents〔ˋpɛrənts〕n. pl. 父母
***help with*** 幫忙　　housework〔ˋhaʊs‚wɜk〕n. 家事
study〔ˋstʌdɪ〕v. 唸書　　exam〔ɪgˋzæm〕n. 考試
***a lot of*** 許多　　***do a lot of studying*** 唸很多書
big〔bɪg〕adj. 重要的
important〔ɪmˋpɔrtṇt〕adj. 重要的

A3：I'd say, "I have an exam tomorrow morning.  It's really important.  Can I help you next time instead?"
我會說：「我明天早上有一個考試。那眞的很重要。我可以下次再幫忙嗎？」

3. Q　：You meet a friend that you have not seen for a long time.  She used to be heavy, but now she is thin.  What do you say to her?　你遇到一個很久沒見的朋友。她以前很胖，但現在她很瘦。你會對她說什麼？

A1：I'd say, "You look great!  I can't believe how much you've changed.  I bet you feel a lot better, too."
我會說：「妳看起來眞棒！我眞無法相信妳變了這麼多。我敢說妳現在一定也感覺很好。」

A2：I'd say, "Wow.  You've really lost weight.  You were always pretty, but now you look fantastic!"
我會說：「哇。妳眞的瘦很多。妳以前就很漂亮了，但現在看起來眞棒！」

【註】 *next time* 下一次　　instead〔ɪnˋstɛd〕adv. 作爲代替
　　　 meet〔mit〕v. 遇見　　long〔lɔŋ〕adj.（時間）長的
　　　 *used to* 以前　　heavy〔ˋhɛvɪ〕adj. 重的
　　　 thin〔θɪn〕adj. 瘦的　　look〔lʊk〕v. 看起來
　　　 believe〔bɪˋliv〕v. 相信　　*how much* 多少
　　　 change〔tʃendʒ〕v. 改變　　bet〔bɛt〕v. 打賭
　　　 *I bet* 我敢說；我確信　　better〔ˋbɛtɚ〕adj. 更好的
　　　 lose〔luz〕v. 減少　　weight〔wet〕n. 重量；體重
　　　 always〔ˋɔlwez〕adv. 總是　　pretty〔ˋprɪtɪ〕adj. 漂亮的
　　　 fantastic〔fænˋtæstɪk〕adj. 極好的；很棒的

**A3**：I'd say, "Hey, you look wonderful!  You must have worked hard to get into such great shape.  You should be proud of yourself."

我會說：「嘿，妳看起來眞棒！妳一定很努力才變成這麼好的身材。妳應該以自己爲榮。」

---

**4. Q** ：You want to go to the library, but you don't know where it is.  Ask someone for help. 你想要去圖書館，但你不知道圖書館在哪裡。請人幫助你。

**A1**："Excuse me.  Can you tell me how to get to the library?  Can I walk there from here?"

「對不起。你可以告訴我圖書館怎麼去嗎？我可以從這裡走去嗎？」

**A2**："Hi.  I'm new here.  I'm looking for the library.  Do you know where it is?"

「嗨。我對這裡不熟。我正在找圖書館。你知道在哪裡嗎？」

【註】 hey〔he〕*interj* 嘿　　wonderful〔'wʌndəfəl〕*adj.* 很棒的
***work hard*** 很努力　　***get into*** 成爲
such〔sʌtʃ〕*adv.* 如此地　　great〔gret〕*adj.* 很棒的
shape〔ʃep〕*n.* 身材　　***be proud of*** 以～爲榮
library〔'laɪ͵brɛrɪ〕*n.* 圖書館　　***get to*** 到達
hi〔haɪ〕*interj.* 嗨　　new〔nju〕*adj.* 新來的；不熟悉的
***look for*** 尋找

**A3**："Hello. Can you help me? I'm trying to get to the library, but I don't know where it is."

「哈囉。你可以幫我嗎？我想去圖書館，但是我不知道圖書館在哪裡。」

---

**5. Q**：You eat lunch in a restaurant. When you want to pay the bill, you find that you forgot to bring your wallet. What would you do?

你在一家餐廳吃午餐。當你要付帳的時候，你發現你忘了帶皮夾。你會怎麼做？

**A1**：I would explain my problem to the manager. Then I would give him my watch to hold. Then I would go to get my wallet.

我會跟經理說明我的問題。接著，我會把我的手錶給他保管。然後我會去拿我的皮夾。

【註】　hello〔hə'lo〕*interj.* 哈囉　　try〔traɪ〕*v.* 嘗試
lunch〔lʌntʃ〕*n.* 午餐　　restaurant〔'rɛstərənt〕*n.* 餐廳
pay〔pe〕*v.* 支付　　bill〔bɪl〕*n.* 帳單
***pay the bill*** 結帳；買單　　forget〔fə'gɛt〕*v.* 忘記
bring〔brɪŋ〕*v.* 帶來　　wallet〔'walɪt〕*n.* 皮夾
explain〔ɪk'splen〕*v.* 解釋；說明
problem〔'prabləm〕*n.* 問題
manager〔'mænɪdʒɚ〕*n.* 經理　　watch〔watʃ〕*n.* 手錶
hold〔hold〕*v.* 保留；擁有　　get〔gɛt〕*v.* 拿

**A2**：I would call my friend. I would say, "Please help me. I'm in a restaurant and I have no money to pay. Can you bring me some cash?"

我會打電話給我的朋友。我會說：「請幫幫我。我在一家餐廳，我沒錢付帳。你可以帶一些現金來給我嗎？」

**A3**：I would apologize to the waiter. Then I would go and get my wallet. I would come back and pay the bill, and I would also give the waiter a big tip.

我會向服務生道歉。然後我會去拿我的皮夾。我會回來付帳，而且我也會給那位服務生一大筆小費。

---

**6. Q**：You want to send a package to Canada. You go to the post office. Find out how much it will cost.

你要寄一個包裹到加拿大。你到郵局去。查出這樣要多少錢。

【註】 call〔kɔl〕v. 打電話給　　cash〔kæʃ〕n. 現金
apologize〔ə'pɑlə‚dʒaɪz〕v. 道歉
waiter〔'wetɚ〕n. 服務生　　tip〔tɪp〕n. 小費
***a big tip*** 一大筆小費　　send〔sɛnd〕v. 寄
package〔'pækɪdʒ〕n. 包裹
Canada〔'kænədə〕n. 加拿大　　***post office*** 郵局
***find out*** 查出　　cost〔kɔst〕v. 花費

**A1**：I would say, "I want to send this to Canada. Can you tell me how much it will cost? Can you give me the price for airmail and surface mail?"

我會說：「我想要寄這個到加拿大。你可以告訴我要多少錢嗎？你可以告訴我航空郵件及普通郵件的價格嗎？」

**A2**：I would say, "I'm sending this to Canada. I'm not sure how much it weighs. Would you please weigh it and tell me what the postage is?"

我會說：「我要將這個寄到加拿大。我不確定它有多重。可以請你稱稱看，然後告訴我郵資是多少嗎？」

**A3**：I would say, "Can you tell me how much the postage will be for this package? I'm sending it to Canada."

我會說：「你可以告訴我這個包裏的郵資是多少嗎？我要寄到加拿大。」

【註】 price〔praɪs〕*n.* 價格　airmail〔'ɛr,mel〕*n.* 航空郵件
surface〔'sɝfɪs〕*adj.* 普通郵件的；陸路郵件的
***surface mail*** 普通平信郵件
sure〔ʃʊr〕*adj.* 確定的　weigh〔we〕*v.* 重～；稱重
postage〔'postɪdʒ〕*n.* 郵資

**7. Q** ： You have just finished a big meal in a restaurant.
The waiter asks if you would like to order dessert.
What do you say?　你在餐廳剛吃完一份大餐。服務
生問你是否要點甜點。你會怎麼說？

**A1** ： I will say, "Oh, I don't think so.　Your food is
delicious, but I'm too full.　I can't eat anymore."
我會說：「喔，我想不要了。你們的餐點很好吃，但是
我太飽了。我沒辦法再吃了。」

**A2** ： I will say, "No, thank you.　I don't have any room
for dessert.　Just the check, please."　我會說：「不
用了，謝謝你。我飽得吃不下甜點。請結帳。」

**A3** ： I will say, "I might.　What do you have?　Can I see
the menu?"　我會說：「我可能會想點。你們有些什麼？
我可以看菜單嗎？」

【註】　finish (ˈfɪnɪʃ) v. 吃完　　big ( bɪg ) adj. 豐盛的
meal ( mil ) n. 一餐　　*would like to V*. 想要…
order (ˈɔrdɚ) v. 點 ( 餐 )
dessert ( dɪˈzɝt ) n. 餐後甜點　　oh ( o ) interj. 喔
*I don't think so*. 我想不是；我想不要了。
delicious ( dɪˈlɪʃəs ) adj. 美味的　　full ( fʊl ) adj. 飽的
*not…anymore* 不再…　　room ( rum ) n. 空間；餘地
check ( tʃɛk ) n. 帳單　　menu (ˈmɛnju ) n. 菜單

*請將下列自我介紹的句子再唸一遍，請開始：

My seat number is <u>（複試座位號碼）</u>, and my test number is
<u>（初試准考證號碼）</u>.

# 初級英語檢定測驗第二階段

# 寫作口說能力測驗⑦

## 寫作能力測驗

本測驗共有兩部份。第一部份為單句寫作,第二部份為段落寫作。測驗時間為 40 分鐘。

### 第一部份:單句寫作

請將答案寫在答案紙上對應的題號旁,如有文法、用字、拼字、標點符號、大小寫等之錯誤,將予扣分。

### 第 1~5 題:句子改寫

請依題目之提示,將原句依指定型式改寫,並將改寫的句子完整地寫在答案紙上。

注意:須寫出提示之文字及標點符號。

例: 題目:I am fine.

She ＿＿＿＿＿＿.

在答案紙上寫:***She is fine.***

1. The repairman is due to come at 10:00.

When ＿＿＿＿＿＿＿＿＿＿＿＿＿＿＿＿＿＿？

2. I gave Mary's pen to Jane.

I gave Jane ＿＿＿＿＿＿＿＿＿＿＿＿＿＿＿＿＿.

3. I was walking my dog at 7:00 last night.

   I _____ right now.

4. Can you tell me where I can find the pickles?

   Where _____?

5. If you win the lottery, will you buy me a car?

   If you won _____?

第 6～10 題：句子合併

　　請依照題目指示，將兩句合併成一句。並將合併的句子完整地寫在答案紙上。

　　注意：須寫出提示之文字及標點符號。

例：題目：John has a cap.

　　　　　The cap is purple.

　　　　　John _____ cap.

　　在答案紙上寫：***John has a purple cap.***

6. This is the best dress.

   I could find it at Macy's.

   This _____ that _____.

7. Martha said she will write the letter.

   She will eat lunch first.

   Martha will _____ after she _____.

8. I didn't read the newspaper.

   I didn't watch the TV news.

   I neither read _____.

9. We were very happy.

   Our team won the game.

   Our team _____, so _____.

10. I cleaned the bathroom this morning.

    My mother told me to do it.

    My mother _____.


第 11～15 題：重組

　　請將題目中所有提示的字詞整合成一有意義的句子，並將重組的
　　句子完整地寫在答案紙上。

　　注意：須寫出提示之文字及標點符號。(答案中必須使用所有提
　　　　　示的字詞，且不能隨意增減字詞，否則不予計分。)

例： 題目：John _____.

　　　　　this morning / late / was / again

　　在答案紙上寫：***John was late again this morning.***

11. Please _____.

    the book / tomorrow / to give / don't / me / forget

12. Have _____?

the parade / start / you / heard / will / when

13. Here is _____.

that / the sandwich / you / ordered

14. You _____.

come / tomorrow / don't / here / early / need to

15. I'll _____.

you / better / turn on / the light / see / so that / can

### 第二部份：段落寫作

題目：上個月，黛安（Diane）和瓊（Joan）去逛街，黛安
拿了兩件洋裝，問瓊的意見。請根據圖片內容寫一篇
約 50 字的簡短描述。

# 口說能力測驗

＊請在 15 秒內完成並唸出下列自我介紹的句子，請開始：

My seat number is （複試座位號碼）, and my test number is
（初試准考證號碼）.

## I. 複誦

共五題。題目不印在試題上，由耳機播出，每題播出兩次，兩
次之間大約有一到二秒的間隔。聽完兩次後，請馬上複誦一次。

## II. 朗讀句子與短文

共有五個句子及一篇短文，請先利用一分鐘的時間閱讀試題上
的句子與短文，然後在一分鐘內以正常的速度，清楚正確的朗
讀一遍。

One : There's a bakery between the post office
and the bank.

Two : Would you mind opening this bag for me?

Three : Unfortunately, the two o'clock show is sold
out.

Four : I'd like to return this shirt.

Five : I read in the newspaper that a typhoon is on
the way.

Six ： Everyone in my family loves amusement parks, and we're going to go to Disney World this summer. My younger sister is especially excited. She loves Mickey, Goofy, and all of the other Disney characters. As for me, I'm excited about the rides. They look really fun. I'm sure we're all going to have a good time.

## III. 回答問題

共七題。題目不印在試題上，由耳機播出，每題播出兩次，兩次之間大約有一到二秒的間隔。聽完兩次後，請馬上回答，每題回答時間為 15 秒，請在作答時間內儘量的表達。

＊請將下列自我介紹的句子再唸一遍，請開始：

My seat number is （複試座位號碼）, and my test number is （初試准考證號碼）.

# 寫作口說能力測驗 ⑦ 詳解

## 寫作能力測驗詳解

### 第一部份：單句寫作

第 1～5 題：句子改寫

1. The repairman is due to come at 10:00.

   When ＿＿＿＿＿＿＿＿＿＿＿＿＿＿＿＿＿＿＿＿＿?

   > 重點結構： 直述句改為疑問句
   >
   > 解　答： <u>When is the repairman due to come?</u>
   >
   > 句型分析： When + be 動詞 + 主詞 + due to + 動詞原形 ?
   >
   > 說　明： 直述句改成 When 的疑問句，將主詞與 be 動詞倒裝，並把句號改成問號。
   >
   > \* repairman〔rɪ'pɛr,mæn〕*n.* 修理人員
   > due〔dju〕*adj.* 預定…的

2. I gave Mary's pen to Jane.

   I gave Jane ＿＿＿＿＿＿＿＿＿＿＿＿＿＿＿＿＿.

   > 重點結構： give 做授與動詞的用法
   >
   > 解　答： <u>I gave Jane Mary's pen.</u>
   >
   > 句型分析： 主詞 + give + 直接受詞（人）+ 間接受詞（物）
   >
   > 說　明： give（給）有兩種用法：
   > $\begin{cases} ① \text{ give} + sb. + sth. \\ ② \text{ give} + sth. + \text{to} + sb. \end{cases}$
   > 本題的用法為第一種。

3. I was walking my dog at 7:00 last night.

   I _____ right now.

   重點結構：現在進行式的用法

   解　答：<u>I am walking my dog right now.</u>

   句型分析：主詞 + be 動詞 + 現在分詞 + 時間副詞

   說　明：時間副詞改爲 right now，表示現在正在進行的動
   作，故動詞時態須改爲「現在進行式」，即「be 動
   詞 + 現在分詞」形式，主詞爲 I，故 be 動詞用 am。

   * walk〔wɔk〕v. 溜（狗）　　***right now*** 現在

4. Can you tell me where I can find the pickles?

   Where _____?

   重點結構：間接問句改爲直接問句

   解　答：<u>Where can I find the pickles?</u>

   句型分析：Where + 助動詞 + 主詞 + 動詞？

   說　明：間接問句與直接問句的差別在於，主詞與 be 動詞或
   助動詞的位置，間接問句的形式爲「疑問詞 + 主詞
   + be 動詞/助動詞」，而直接問句的形式爲「疑問詞 +
   be 動詞/助動詞 + 主詞」，本句的意思爲「我可以在
   哪裡找到泡菜？」

   * pickles〔ˈpɪk!z〕n. pl. 泡菜

5. If you win the lottery, will you buy me a car?

   If you won _____?

   重點結構：過去式條件句

解　答：<u>If you won the lottery, would you buy me a car?</u>

句型分析：If＋主詞＋過去式動詞＋,＋過去式助動詞＋主詞
　　　　　＋原形動詞？

說　明：本句句意原為「如果你贏得樂透，你會買一輛車給
　　　　我嗎？」，為未來式直說法，由句首改成 If you won
　　　　可知，本句要改成條件句的過去式，故主要子句的
　　　　助動詞，須用過去式 would。

＊ win〔wɪn〕v. 贏得　　　lottery〔ˈlɑtərɪ〕n. 樂透；彩券

第 6～10 題：句子合併

6. This is the best dress.

I could find it at Macy's.

This ＿＿＿＿＿＿＿＿＿＿＿ that ＿＿＿＿＿＿＿＿＿＿＿.

重點結構：that 引導形容詞子句的用法

解　答：<u>This is the best dress that I could find at Macy's.</u>

句型分析：This is＋主詞補語＋that＋主詞＋助動詞＋動詞＋
　　　　　地方副詞

說　明：that 在此為關係代名詞，代替先行詞 the best dress，
　　　　引導形容詞子句，句意是「這件是我在梅西百貨所能
　　　　找到最好的衣服了，故主要子句 This is the best
　　　　dress 放在 that 之前，形容詞子句 I could find at
　　　　Macy's 放在 that 之後。

＊ dress〔drɛs〕n. 衣服；洋裝
　**Macy's** 梅西百貨【美國一間大型百貨公司】

7. Martha said she will write the letter.

She will eat lunch first.

Martha will ＿＿＿＿＿＿＿＿ after she ＿＿＿＿＿＿＿＿．

重點結構：after 的用法

解　答：Martha will write the letter after she eats lunch.

句型分析：主詞 + 助動詞 + 動詞 + after + 主詞 + 動詞

說　明：由副詞 first（先）可知，瑪莎會先吃午餐，再寫
信，用 after「在～之後」來表示事情的先後順序。
故先寫 write the letter，再寫 eat lunch。又 after
所引導的為表「時間」的副詞子句，不可用 will，
要用現在式代替未來式，主詞 Martha 為第三人稱
單數，故 eat 要加 s。

8. I didn't read the newspaper.

I didn't watch the TV news.

I neither read ＿＿＿＿＿＿＿＿＿＿＿＿＿＿＿＿＿＿．

重點結構：「neither…nor～」的用法

解　答：I neither read the newspaper nor watched the
TV news.

句型分析：主詞 + neither + A + nor + B

說　明：「neither…nor～」為對等連接詞，用來連接文法
作用相同的單字、片語或子句，本身已有否定的意
思，故用在肯定的句型中，在此是用來連接二個動
詞，即 read the newspaper 和 watch the TV news，
又提示中的時態為過去式，故動詞時態改為過去式。

* read〔rid〕v. 閱讀【三態變化為：read-read〔rɛd〕-read〔rɛd〕】
newspaper〔'njuz,pepɚ〕n. 報紙　　news〔njuz〕n. 新聞

9. We were very happy.

Our team won the game.

Our team _____ , so _____ .

重點結構：so 的用法

解　答：Our team won the game, so we were very happy.

句型分析：主詞＋動詞＋, ＋ so ＋主詞＋ be 動詞＋形容詞

説　明：連接詞 so（所以）和 because（因為）的比較：

{ 原因＋, so ＋結果

{ 結果＋ because ＋原因

原因是「我們這一隊贏得比賽」，結果是「我們非常高興」，把原因放在 so 之前，結果放在 so 之後。

＊ team〔tim〕n. 隊

　 win〔wɪn〕v. 贏得【三態變化為：win-won-won】

　 game〔gem〕n. 比賽

10. I cleaned the bathroom this morning.

My mother told me to do it.

My mother _____ _____ .

重點結構：tell 的用法

解　答：My mother told me to clean the bathroom this morning.

句型分析：主詞＋ tell ＋受詞＋ to V. ＋時間副詞

説　明：tell 的用法為：「tell *sb.* to V.」表示「告訴某人去做～」，本題的意思為「我媽媽今天早上叫我去打掃廁所」。

＊ clean〔klin〕v. 打掃　　　bathroom〔'bæθ,rum〕n. 浴室；廁所

第 11～15 題：重組

11. Please _____.

    the book / tomorrow / to give / don't / me / forget

    重點結構：祈使句的用法

     解　答：<u>Please don't forget to give me the book tomorrow.</u>

    句型分析：Please ＋ 動詞否定 ＋ to V. ＋ 時間副詞

     說　明：此題為祈使句的否定句型，Please 後面須接原形動
        詞的否定形式 don't forget，forget 後面接不定詞，
        表「忘記做～」，句意為「明天請別忘了帶那本書給
        我」。

12. Have _____?

    the parade / start / you / heard / will / when

    重點結構：間接問句的用法

     解　答：<u>Have you heard when the parade will start?</u>

    句型分析：Have you heard ＋ when ＋ 主詞 ＋ 動詞？

     說　明：題目由助動詞 have 開頭，而提示中有疑問詞 when，
        可得知本題是考間接問句的用法，由疑問詞引導的子
        句做為間接問句，即「疑問詞 ＋ 主詞 ＋ 動詞」的形式，
        作為 Have you heard 的受詞，句意為「你有聽到遊
        行什麼時候開始嗎？」」

    * parade〔pə'red〕n. 遊行　　start〔stɑrt〕v. 開始

13. Here is _____.

    that / the sandwich / you / ordered

    重點結構：that 引導形容詞子句

解　答：<u>Here is the sandwich that you ordered.</u>

句型分析：Here + be 動詞 + 主詞 + that + 主詞 + 動詞

說　明：that 在這裡當關係代名詞，引導形容詞子句，即「關代 + 主詞 + 動詞」，修飾先行詞，故 Here is 後面接主詞 the sandwich，再寫 that 子句。本句的意思為「這是您點的三明治」。

\* sandwich (ˈsændwɪtʃ) *n.* 三明治　　order (ˈɔrdɚ) *v.* 點 ( 餐 )

14. You _____.

come / tomorrow / don't / here / early / need to

重點結構：句子基本結構

解　答：<u>You don't need to come here early tomorrow.</u>

句型分析：主詞 + 動詞否定 + to V. + 時間副詞

說　明：本句的意思是「你明天不需要太早來這裡」，主詞 you 後面接動詞的否定形式 don't need，to come here early 為不定詞片語，放在動詞後，tomorrow 為時間副詞，放在句尾。

\* early (ˈɝlɪ) *adv.* 早

15. I'll _____.

you / better / turn on / the light / see / so that / can

重點結構：so that 的用法

解　答：<u>I'll turn on the light so that you can see better.</u>

句型分析：主詞 + 助動詞 + 動詞 + so that + 主詞 + can/could /may/might/will/would + 原形動詞

説　明：so that（以便；為了）是一表「目的」的從屬連接
　　　　　詞，其所引導的副詞子句中，必須要有如上列的助
　　　　　動詞之一，且該子句只能放在主要子句之後。依句
　　　　　意，「我會把燈打開，這樣你可以看得更清楚。」

* **turn on** 打開　　　light〔laɪt〕*n.* 燈
　**see better** 看得更清楚

## 第二部份：段落寫作

### 【作文範例】

　　Diane and Joan went shopping **last month**. Diane
wanted to buy a new dress. She found two that she liked.
She asked Joan which one was better. Joan chose the dress
with polka dots. Diane thanked her and went to pay for the
dress. But she did not buy the polka dot dress. She bought
the other one! Diane thought that Joan did not dress well.
Joan was very angry.

* shop〔ʃɑp〕*v.* 購物　　　**last month** 上個月
　want〔wɑnt〕*v.* 想要　　　dress〔drɛs〕*n.* 洋裝　*v.* 穿衣服
　find〔faɪnd〕*v.* 找到　　　like〔laɪk〕*v.* 喜歡
　ask〔æsk〕*v.* 問　　　choose〔tʃuz〕*v.* 選擇
　dot〔dɑt〕*n.* 點　　　**polka dot** 圓點花樣
　thank〔θæŋk〕*v.* 感謝　　　**pay for** 支付～的錢
　**the other one** 另一個　　　think〔θɪŋk〕*v.* 認為
　well〔wɛl〕*adv.* 良好地　　　angry〔'æŋgrɪ〕*adj.* 生氣的

# 口說能力測驗詳解

＊請在15秒內完成並唸出下列自我介紹的句子，請開始：

My seat number is （複試座位號碼）, and my test number is （初試准考證號碼）.

## I. 複誦

共五題。題目不印在試題上，由耳機播出，每題播出兩次，兩次之間大約有一到二秒的間隔。聽完兩次後，請馬上複誦一次。

1. John likes to read comic books. 約翰喜歡看漫畫。

2. Have you seen the movie? 你看過這部電影了嗎？

3. Please wait a minute. 請等一下。

4. The book is on my desk. 那本書在我的書桌上。

5. The meal was delicious. 這一餐相當美味。

【註】 ***comic book*** 漫畫書
movie (ˈmuvɪ) *n.* 電影
wait ( wet ) *v.* 等
minute (ˈmɪnɪt) *n.* 分鐘
***wait a minute*** 等一下
desk ( dɛsk ) *n.* 書桌
meal ( mil ) *n.* 一餐
delicious ( dɪˈlɪʃəs ) *adj.* 美味的

## II. 朗讀句子與短文

共有五個句子及一篇短文，請先利用一分鐘的時間閱讀試題上的句子與短文，然後在一分鐘內以正常的速度，清楚正確的朗讀一遍。

One : There's a bakery between the post office and the bank. 郵局和銀行中間有一家麵包店。

Two : Would you mind opening this bag for me? 你介意為我打開這個袋子嗎？

Three : Unfortunately, the two o'clock show is sold out. 遺憾的是，兩點的表演門票已經賣完了。

Four : I'd like to return this shirt. 我想要退還這件襯衫。

Five : I read in the newspaper that a typhoon is on the way. 我從報紙上得知，有一個颱風正在接近當中。

【註】 bakery (ˈbekərɪ) n. 麵包店
between (bəˈtwin) prep. 在 ( 兩者 ) 之間
*post office* 郵局    bank (bæŋk) n. 銀行
mind (maɪnd) v. 介意    open (ˈopən) v. 打開
bag (bæg) n. 袋子
unfortunately (ʌnˈfɔrtʃənɪtlɪ) adv. 不幸地；遺憾地
show (ʃo) n. 表演    *the two o'clock show* 兩點的表演
*sell out* 賣完    *would like* 想要
return (rɪˈtɜn) v. 退還    shirt (ʃɜt) n. 襯衫
newspaper (ˈnjuzˌpepə) n. 報紙
typhoon (taɪˈfun) n. 颱風    *on the way* 在進行中；接近

Six : Everyone in my family loves amusement parks, and we're going to go to Disney World this summer. My younger sister is especially excited. She loves Mickey, Goofy, and all the other Disney characters. As for me, I'm excited about the rides. They look really fun. I'm sure we're all going to have a good time.

我們家的每個人都愛遊樂園，我們今年夏天將要去迪士尼樂園。我妹妹特別興奮。她很喜愛米奇、高飛，和所有其它迪士尼的人物。至於我，我對遊樂設施很感興趣。它們看起來眞的很有趣。我確信我們會玩得很愉快。

【註】 love〔lʌv〕v. 喜愛
amusement〔ə'mjuzmənt〕n. 娛樂
*amusement park* 遊樂園
*Disney World* 迪士尼樂園
summer〔'sʌmɚ〕n. 夏天　　*younger sister* 妹妹
especially〔ə'spɛʃəlɪ〕adv. 尤其；特別地
excited〔ɪk'saɪtɪd〕adj. 興奮的
*Mickey* 米老鼠；米奇　　*Goofy* 高飛
*the other* 其他的　　character〔'kærɪktɚ〕n. 人物
*as for* 至於　　*be excited about* 對⋯很感興趣
ride〔raɪd〕n. 遊樂設施　　look〔luk〕v. 看起來
really〔'rɪəlɪ〕adv. 眞地　　fun〔fʌn〕adj. 有趣的
sure〔ʃur〕adj. 確信的　　*have a good time* 玩得很愉快

## III. 回答問題

共七題。題目不印在試題上，由耳機播出，每題播出兩次，兩次之間大約有一到二秒的間隔。聽完兩次後，請馬上回答，每題回答時間為 15 秒，請在作答時間內儘量的表達。

**1. Q** : You borrowed 500 dollars from your friend yesterday. Now you are giving the money back. What do you say to your friend?

你昨天向你的朋友借了五百元。現在你要把錢還給他。你會對你的朋友說什麼？

**A1** : I'd say, "Here's that money you gave me yesterday. Thanks again for your help. I really appreciated the loan." 我會說：「這是你昨天借我的錢。再次謝謝你的幫忙。我真的很感激你借我錢。」

**A2** : I'd say, "You really saved my life yesterday. Here is that 500 you loaned me. If there is anything I can do for you, just ask."

我會說：「昨天你真的救了我一命。這是你借我的五百元。如果有什麼我可以為你效勞的，儘管開口。」

【註】 borrow〔'baro〕v. 借（入）

***give sth. back*** 歸還某物

again〔ə'gɛn〕adv. 再一次　　　help〔hɛlp〕n. 幫忙

appreciate〔ə'priʃɪˌet〕v. 感激

loan〔lon〕n. 借款　v. 借（錢）　　save〔sev〕v. 拯救

life〔laɪf〕n. 生命　　ask〔æsk〕v. 要求

**A3**：I'd say, "Thanks a lot for your help yesterday.
Here is what I borrowed.  Can you check it and
make sure it's all there?"

我會說：「非常謝謝你昨天的幫忙。這是我借的錢。
可以請你檢查一下，並確認金額是否正確？」

2. **Q**　：You have a terrible cold.  You go to the doctor
and he asks you what is wrong.  What do you say?

你得了重感冒。你去看醫生，他問你哪裡不舒服。
你會怎麼說？

**A1**：I will say, "I feel terrible.  My head aches and I
can't stop coughing.  Besides that, my throat is
sore."  我會說：「我感覺糟透了。我的頭很痛，而且
一直咳嗽。除此之外，我的喉嚨很痛。」

【註】　check ( tʃɛk ) v. 檢查　　***make sure*** 確定；確認
　　***make sure it's all there*** 確認金額是否正確 ( = *make sure*
　　　*that the amount is correct* )
　　terrible ('tɛrəbḷ ) adj. 嚴重的；難受的
　　cold ( kold ) n. 感冒　　***go to the doctor*** 去看醫生
　　wrong ( rɔŋ ) adj. 不舒服的　　feel ( fil ) v. 感覺
　　head ( hɛd ) n. 頭　　ache ( ek ) v. 疼痛
　　stop ( stɑp ) v. 停止　　cough ( kɔf ) v. 咳嗽
　　besides ( bɪ'saɪdz ) prep. 除了…之外
　　throat ( θrot ) n. 喉嚨　　sore ( sor ) adj. 痛的

**A2** : I will say, "I have had a cold for three days now.
I really feel bad. Can you give me something to
make me feel better?"

我會說：「我已經感冒三天了。我真的覺得很不舒服。
你可以給我些什麼讓我感覺舒服一點嗎？」

**A3** : I will say, "I have a runny nose and a sore throat.
I'm also coughing so much that I can't sleep at
night. What can I do?"

我會說：「我流鼻水而且喉嚨痛。我也咳嗽得很嚴重，
以致於晚上都睡不著。我該怎麼辦？」

---

**3. Q** : You are studying and your roommate is listening
to the radio. You cannot concentrate. What do
you do? 你正在唸書，而你的室友正在聽廣播。
你沒辦法專心。你會怎麼辦？

【註】 bad〔bæd〕*adj.* 很糟的　　make〔mek〕*v.* 使
better〔'bɛtɚ〕*adj.* 較好的
runny〔'rʌnɪ〕*adj.*（鼻、眼）分泌液體的
nose〔noz〕*n.* 鼻子　　***have a runny nose*** 流鼻水
sleep〔slip〕*v.* 睡覺　　study〔'stʌdɪ〕*v.* 讀書
roommate〔'rum‚met〕*n.* 室友
***listen to*** 聽　　radio〔'redɪ‚o〕*n.* 廣播
concentrate〔'kɑnsn‚tret〕*v.* 專心

**A1**：I would ask him to lower the volume.　I think he would understand.　After all, he also has to study sometimes.　我會請他降低音量。我想他會了解。畢竟，他有時也必須讀書。

**A2**：I would say, "Could you turn that off or use your earphones?　I'm trying to study.　I can't read and listen to music at the same time."
我會說：「你可以把廣播關掉，或使用耳機嗎？我想唸書。我無法同時讀書和聽音樂。」

**A3**：I would take my books and go to the library.　It's his room, too.　He has the right to listen to music if he wants to.
我會帶著我的書到圖書館。這也是他的房間。如果他想要的話，他有聽音樂的權利。

【註】 lower〔'loɚ〕v. 降低　　volume〔'valjəm〕n. 音量
understand〔ˌʌndɚ'stænd〕v. 了解
*after all* 畢竟　　sometimes〔'sʌmˌtaɪmz〕adv. 有時候
*turn off* 關掉　　use〔juz〕v. 使用
earphones〔'ɪrˌfonz〕n. pl. 耳機
*try to* 試著；想要　　music〔'mjuzɪk〕n. 音樂
*at the same time* 同時　　take〔tek〕v. 帶
library〔'laɪˌbrɛrɪ〕n. 圖書館
room〔rum〕n. 房間　　right〔raɪt〕n. 權利
want〔wɑnt〕v. 想要

**4. Q**：You receive a phone call. The caller wants to
speak to Mary, but you don't know anyone named
Mary. What do you say?
你接到一通電話。打電話來的人想和瑪麗說話，
但是你不認識任何叫瑪麗的人。你會怎麼說？

**A1**：I would say, "I'm sorry, but you have the wrong
number. There is no one called Mary here."
我會說：「抱歉，你打錯了。這裡沒有叫瑪麗的人。」

**A2**：I would say, "I think you called the wrong number.
What number are you trying to reach? No, that's
not my number." 我會說：「我想你打錯電話了。
你是要打幾號呢？不是，那不是我的電話號碼。」

**A3**：I would say, "No, this isn't Mary's number. I
don't know who she is. I hope you find her!"
我會說：「不是，這不是瑪麗的電話號碼。我不知道
她是誰。我希望你能夠找到她！」

【註】 receive ( rɪ'siv ) v. 接到　　phone ( fon ) n. 電話
　　　*a phone call* 一通電話　　caller ('kɔlɚ ) n. 打電話的人
　　　speak ( spik ) v. 說話　　*named* ~ 名叫~
　　　wrong ( rɔŋ ) adj. 錯誤的
　　　number ('nʌmbɚ ) n. 電話號碼
　　　*You have the wrong number.* 你打錯電話了。
　　　*called* ~ 叫做~　　reach ( ritʃ ) v. 連絡
　　　hope ( hop ) v. 希望　　find ( faɪnd ) v. 找到

**5. Q** : A stranger asks you where the post office is.
It is in the next block.  Give him directions.

一位陌生人問你郵局在哪裡。郵局在下一個街區。
給他一點指示。

**A1** : I would say, "The post office is very close.  Just
walk straight ahead, cross the street, and then
you will see it on your right."

我會說：「郵局離這裡非常近。只要直直地向前走，
穿過街道，然後你就會看到郵局在你的右邊。」

**A2** : I would say, "It's not far.  It's just in the next
block.  I'm going that way, so I can show you
if you like."

我會說：「郵局不會很遠。它就在下一個街區。我正要
往那個方向，所以如果你想要的話，我可以帶你去。」

【註】 stranger〔'strendʒɚ〕n. 陌生人
next〔nɛkst〕adj. 下一個的　　block〔blɑk〕n. 街區
directions〔də'rɛkʃənz〕n. pl. 指示
close〔klos〕adj. 接近的　　straight〔stret〕adv. 直直地
ahead〔ə'hɛd〕adv. 向前方　　cross〔krɔs〕v. 穿越
street〔strit〕n. 街道　　right〔raɪt〕n. 右邊
far〔fɑr〕adj. 遙遠的　　just〔dʒʌst〕adv. 就
way〔we〕n. 方向　　show〔ʃo〕v. 帶領
like〔laɪk〕v. 想要；願意

**A3**: I would say, "It's just one block that way. You'll see it on your right. You can't miss it."

我會說：「郵局就在那個方向的下一個街區。你會看到它在你的右邊。你不可能會錯過的。」

---

**6. Q** : Your friend is sick. You visit your friend and bring a gift for him or her. What do you say?

你的朋友生病了。你去探望你的朋友，並帶禮物給他（她）。你會說什麼？

**A1**: I would say, "I'm so sorry that you're not feeling well. These flowers are for you. I hope they cheer you up."

我會說：「我很遺憾你身體不舒服。這些花是給你的。我希望它們能夠讓你打起精神。」

【註】 miss〔mɪs〕v. 錯過　　sick〔sɪk〕adj. 生病的
　　　 visit〔'vɪzɪt〕v. 探望（病人）
　　　 bring〔brɪŋ〕v. 帶　　gift〔gɪft〕n. 禮物
　　　 sorry〔'sɔrɪ〕adj. 遺憾的；感到難過的
　　　 well〔wɛl〕adj. 好的；健康的
　　　 flower〔'flauɚ〕n. 花
　　　 *cheer sb. up* 使某人振作起來

**A2**：I would say, "I'm sorry you're sick.  I hope you get well soon.  Here is a little something to make you feel better."

我會說：「我很遺憾你生病了。我希望你能早日康復。這是一點小東西，是要讓你心情好一點的。」

**A3**：I would say, "How terrible that you have to stay in bed!  You must be so bored.  I thought you might like some magazines.  Get well soon!"

我會說：「真是糟糕，你必須待在床上！你一定覺得很無聊吧。我覺得你應該會想看幾本雜誌。祝你早日康復！」

---

**7. Q**：Your friend invites you to a concert, but you already have other plans.  What do you say?

你的朋友邀請你去一場音樂會，但是你已經有別的計畫了。你會怎麼說？

【註】 ***get well*** 康復　　soon〔sun〕*adv.* 很快地
***a little something*** 一點小東西
terrible〔'tɛrəbl〕*adj.* 糟糕的
***stay in bed*** 待在床上　　bored〔bord〕*adj.* 無聊的
magazine〔͵mægə'zin〕*n.* 雜誌
invite〔ɪn'vaɪt〕*v.* 邀請　　concert〔'kɑnsɝt〕*n.* 音樂會
already〔ɔl'rɛdɪ〕*adv.* 已經
other〔'ʌðɚ〕*adj.* 其他的　　plan〔plæn〕*n.* 計畫

**A1**：I would say, "Oh, I wish I could go!  Unfortunately, I already have plans on that night.  But thank you very much for inviting me."

我會說：「喔，我真希望我可以去！遺憾的是，那天晚上我已經有別的計畫了。但還是非常謝謝你邀請我。」

**A2**：I would say, "Thank you so much.  It sounds like fun.  But I'm afraid I can't go.  Let's do something else together soon."

我會說：「非常感謝你。聽起來很有趣。但是恐怕我不能去。我們近期內再一起做些什麼吧。」

**A3**：I would say, "It's so nice of you to ask.  I wish I could go, but I'm busy that night.  Have a good time!" 我會說：「你人真好，會邀請我。真希望我可以去，但是我那天晚上很忙。祝你玩得愉快！」

【註】 oh〔o〕*interj.* 喔    wish〔wɪʃ〕*v.* 希望
unfortunately〔ʌn'fɔtʃənɪtlɪ〕*adv.* 不幸地；遺憾地
sound〔saʊnd〕*v.* 聽起來    fun〔fʌn〕*n.* 有趣
afraid〔ə'fred〕*adj.* 恐怕…的    else〔ɛls〕*adj.* 其他的
together〔tə'gɛðɚ〕*adv.* 一起    nice〔naɪs〕*adj.* 好的
ask〔æsk〕*v.* 邀請    busy〔'bɪzɪ〕*adj.* 忙碌的
***Have a good time.*** 祝你玩得愉快。

\* 請將下列自我介紹的句子再唸一遍，請開始：

My seat number is <u>（複試座位號碼）</u>, and my test number is <u>（初試准考證號碼）</u>.

# 初級英語檢定測驗第二階段

# 寫作口說能力測驗⑧

## 寫作能力測驗

本測驗共有兩部份。第一部份為單句寫作,第二部份為段落寫作。測驗時間為 40 分鐘。

### 第一部份:單句寫作

請將答案寫在答案紙上對應的題號旁,如有文法、用字、拼字、標點符號、大小寫等之錯誤,將予扣分。

第 1~5 題:句子改寫

請依題目之提示,將原句依指定型式改寫,並將改寫的句子<u>完整</u>地寫在答案紙上。

注意:須寫出提示之文字及標點符號。

例: 題目:I am fine.

She ＿＿＿＿＿＿＿.

在答案紙上寫:***She is fine.***

1. The news is on channel 4 at 10:00.

   What ＿＿＿＿＿＿＿＿＿＿＿＿＿＿＿＿＿ 10:00?

2. Did you go to the museum today?

   You ＿＿＿＿＿＿＿＿＿＿＿＿＿＿＿＿＿, didn't you?

3. Steven named his dog Spot.

Who _____?

4. My sister goes to a swimming class every day.

My sister _____ yesterday.

5. Tell me what you saw at the zoo.

What _____?

第 6～10 題：句子合併

　　請依照題目指示，將兩句合併成一句。並將合併的句子完整地寫在答案紙上。

　　注意：須寫出提示之文字及標點符號。

例：　題目：John has a cap.

　　　　　The cap is purple.

　　　　　John _____ cap.

　　在答案紙上寫：***John has a purple cap***.

6. I like strawberry ice cream.

I don't like chocolate ice cream.

I like _____.

7. Will you lend me 100 dollars?

I promise to give it back tomorrow.

If _____?

8. The speech was so boring.

I fell asleep.

The speech was so _____.

9. I would buy a car.

I won the lottery.

If _____.

10. Jessie made rice for dinner.

Jessie made chicken for dinner.

Jessie made _____.

第 11～15 題：重組

　　請將題目中所有提示的字詞整合成一有意義的句子，並將重組的
　　句子完整地寫在答案紙上。

　　注意：　須寫出提示之文字及標點符號。(答案中必須使用所有提
　　　　　　示的字詞，且不能隨意增減字詞，否則不予計分。)

例：　題目：John _____.

　　　　　this morning / late / was / again

　　在答案紙上寫：***John was late again this morning.***

11. The _____.

town / train / does not / at / express / every / stop

12. The best way _____.

 to take / number / is / to get to / 32 / the stadium / bus

13. Larry _____.

 neither / a car / can / ride / a bike / drive / nor

14. Did _____?

 go to / Mary and John / alone / the park

15. We won't be able to see _____.

 electricity / there is / no / if

**第二部份：段落寫作**

 題目： 昨天溫蒂（Wendy）在公園等她的男朋友提姆（Tim），
 被提姆從背後嚇了一大跳。請根據圖片內容寫一篇約50
 字的簡短描述。

# 口說能力測驗

＊請在15秒內完成並唸出下列自我介紹的句子，請開始：

My seat number is （複試座位號碼）, and my test number is （初試准考證號碼）.

## I. 複誦

共五題。題目不印在試題上，由耳機播出，每題播出兩次，兩次之間大約有一到二秒的間隔。聽完兩次後，請馬上複誦一次。

## II. 朗讀句子與短文

共有五個句子及一篇短文，請先利用一分鐘的時間閱讀試題上的句子與短文，然後在一分鐘內以正常的速度，清楚正確的朗讀一遍。

One : I'll go to the market to buy some fruit.

Two : That test was the hardest one yet.

Three : Is that order for here or to go?

Four : It usually rains a lot in April.

Five : I met a very interesting man at John's party yesterday.

Six ： My favorite hobby is swimming.  I learned to
swim when I was very young, so I've always
been comfortable in the water.  I usually swim
at the public pool down the street.  It's never
too crowded and it's not expensive.  Next year,
I plan to join the swim team at my high school.
I hope I'm good enough to make it!

## III. 回答問題

共七題。題目不印在試題上，由耳機播出，每題播出兩次，兩
次之間大約有一到二秒的間隔。聽完兩次後，請馬上回答，每
題回答時間為 15 秒，請在作答時間內儘量的表達。

＊請將下列自我介紹的句子再唸一遍，請開始：

My seat number is （複試座位號碼）, and my test number is
（初試准考證號碼）.

# 寫作口説能力測驗 ⑧ 詳解

## 寫作能力測驗詳解

### 第一部份：單句寫作

第 1~5 題：句子改寫

1. The news is on channel 4 at 10:00.

   What _____ 10:00?

   > 重點結構：直述句改爲疑問句
   >
   > 解　答：<u>What is on channel 4 at 10:00?</u>
   >
   > 句型分析：What + 動詞 + 時間副詞？
   >
   > 説　明：疑問詞 What 在此爲疑問代名詞，做主詞用，故後面直接接動詞，並把句號改成問號即可。
   >
   > * on〔ɑn〕adv. 在播放　　channel〔'tʃænḷ〕n. 頻道

2. Did you go to the museum today?

   You _____, didn't you?

   > 重點結構：附加問句的用法
   >
   > 解　答：<u>You went to the museum today, didn't you?</u>
   >
   > 句型分析：主詞 + 動詞（肯定）+ , + 否定助動詞的縮寫 + 人稱代名詞？
   >
   > 説　明：這題的意思是「你今天去了博物館，不是嗎？」附加問句中的助動詞是否定，則敘述句的動詞應用肯定，又因是過去式，故將 go to 改爲 went to。
   >
   > * museum〔mju'ziəm〕n. 博物館

3. Steven named his dog Spot.

Who _____?

重點結構：直述句改為疑問句

解　答：<u>Who named his dog Spot?</u>

句型分析：Who + 動詞 + 受詞？

説　明：疑問詞 Who 在此為疑問代名詞，做主詞用，故後面直接接動詞，並把句號改成問號。

* name〔nem〕v. 為…取名　　spot〔spɑt〕n. 斑點

4. My sister goes to a swimming class every day.

My sister _____ yesterday.

重點結構：過去式動詞

解　答：<u>My sister went to a swimming class yesterday.</u>

句型分析：主詞 + 過去式動詞 + 時間副詞

説　明：提示中的時間副詞為 yesterday，動詞須用過去式表達「過去時間的動作」，故 goes to 須改成 went to。

* swimming〔'swɪmɪŋ〕n. 游泳　　***go to a~class*** 去上～課

5. Tell me what you saw at the zoo.

What _____?

重點結構：間接問句改直接問句

解　答：<u>What did you see at the zoo?</u>

句型分析：What + 助動詞 + 主詞 + 原形動詞 + 地方副詞？

　　説　明：間接問句與直接問句的差別在於,主詞與 be 動詞或
　　　　　　助動詞的位置,本題改為直接問句,即「疑問詞＋
　　　　　　be 動詞/助動詞＋主詞」的形式,故須在疑問詞 what
　　　　　　與主詞 you 之間加助動詞,依提示時態為過去式,
　　　　　　故加 did,而動詞 saw 改為原形 see。

＊ zoo〔zu〕 *n.* 動物園

## 第6～10題：句子合併

6. I like strawberry ice cream.

I don't like chocolate ice cream.

I like _____.

重點結構：but 的用法

　解　答：I like strawberry ice cream, but I don't like
　　　　　chocolate (ice cream).

　　　或 I like strawberry ice cream, but not chocolate
　　　　 (ice cream).

句型分析：主詞＋動詞＋A＋, ＋but＋主詞＋動詞否定＋B
　　　或 主詞＋動詞＋A＋, ＋but＋not＋B

　説　明：依句意,「我喜歡草莓冰淇淋,但是我不喜歡巧克力
　　　　　冰淇淋」,用反義連接詞 but,來連接前後所說意義
　　　　　恰好相反或相互對比的句子,也可把相同的主詞 I
　　　　　和助動詞 do 省略。

＊ strawberry〔'strɔ,bɛrɪ〕 *n.* 草莓
　ice cream〔'aɪs'krim〕 *n.* 冰淇淋
　chocolate〔'tʃɔkəlɪt〕 *n.* 巧克力

7. Will you lend me 100 dollars?

I promise to give it back tomorrow.

If _____?

重點結構：if 條件句

解　答：<u>If I promise to give it back tomorrow, will you lend me 100 dollars?</u>

句型分析：If＋主詞＋動詞＋, ＋助動詞＋主詞＋原形動詞？

說　明：本題的意思為「如果我保證明天把錢還給你，你會借我一百元嗎？」if 後面應接表「條件」的副詞子句，故先寫 I promise to give it back tomorrow，再寫主要子句 will you lend me 100 dollars。當 if 放在句首時，條件子句和主要子句之間須加一個逗號。

＊ lend〔lɛnd〕v. 借（出）　　promise〔'prɑmɪs〕v. 保證

**give sth. back** 歸還某物

8. The speech was so boring.

I fell asleep.

The speech was so _____.

重點結構：「so…that～」的用法

解　答：<u>The speech was so boring that I fell asleep.</u>

句型分析：主詞＋be 動詞＋so＋形容詞＋that＋主詞＋動詞

說　明：這題的意思是說「這場演講太無聊，所以我睡著了」，用「so…that～」合併兩句，表「如此…以致於～」。

＊ speech〔spitʃ〕n. 演講　　boring〔'borɪŋ〕adj. 無聊的

**fall asleep** 睡著

9. I would buy a car.

   I won the lottery.

   If _____.

   　重點結構：if 條件句

   　解　答：<u>If I won the lottery, I would buy a car.</u>

   　句型分析：If＋主詞＋動詞＋,＋主詞＋助動詞＋原形動詞

   　說　明：本題的意思為「如果我中樂透，我就會買一輛車」，
   　　　　　if 後面應接表「條件」的副詞子句，故先寫 I won
   　　　　　the lottery，再寫主要子句 I would buy a car。當
   　　　　　if 放在句首時，條件子句和主要子句之間須加一個
   　　　　　逗號。

   　＊ lottery〔ˈlɑtərɪ〕*n.* 樂透；彩券

10. Jessie made rice for dinner.

    Jessie made chicken for dinner.

    Jessie made _____.

    　重點結構：and 的用法

    　解　答：<u>Jessie made rice and chicken for dinner.</u>
    　　　或 <u>Jessie made chicken and rice for dinner.</u>

    　句型分析：主詞＋動詞＋A＋and＋B＋介系詞片語

    　說　明：連接詞 and（和）為對等連接詞，須連接前後文法
    　　　　　功能相同的單字、片語或句子，此題的 and 連接二
    　　　　　個名詞，即 rice 和 chicken。

    　＊ make〔mek〕*v.* 準備；烹製（飯菜）　　　rice〔raɪs〕*n.* 米飯
    　　chicken〔ˈtʃɪkɪn〕*n.* 雞肉

**第 11～15 題：重組**

11. The _____.

town / train / does not / at / express / every / stop

重點結構：句子基本結構

解　答：<u>The express train does not stop at every town.</u>

句型分析：主詞 + 動詞否定 + 地方副詞

説　明：本句的意思是「特快車不是每個城鎮都會停」，先找
　　　　出主詞 the express train，does not stop 為動詞否
　　　　定，放在主詞後，at every town 為地方副詞，放在
　　　　句尾。

＊ express〔ɪkˈsprɛs〕*adj.* 快速的　　***express train*** 特快車
　　stop〔stɑp〕*v.* 停　　town〔taʊn〕*n.* 城鎮

12. The best way _____.

to take / number / is / to get to / 32 / the stadium / bus

重點結構：句子基本結構

解　答：<u>The best way to get to the stadium is to take</u>
　　　　<u>bus number 32.</u>

句型分析：主詞 + be 動詞 + to V.

説　明：這題的意思是說「到體育館最好的方法是搭 32 號公
　　　　車」，主詞為 The best way to get to the stadium，
　　　　後面接 be 動詞 is，再接不定詞 to take bus number
　　　　32 當主詞補語。

＊ best〔bɛst〕*adj.* 最好的　　way〔we〕*n.* 方法
　　***get to*** 到達　　stadium〔ˈstedɪəm〕*n.* 體育館
　　take〔tek〕*v.* 搭乘　　number〔ˈnʌmbɚ〕*n.* 第…號

13. Larry _____.

neither / a car / can / ride / a bike / drive / nor

　　重點結構：「neither…nor~」的用法

　　　解　答：Larry can neither drive a car nor ride a bike.

　　　　　　或 Larry can neither ride a bike nor drive a car.

　　句型分析：主詞 + 助動詞 + neither + A + nor + B

　　　說　明：「neither…nor~」為對等連接詞，用來連接文法
　　　　　　　作用相同的單字、片語或子句，本身已有否定的意
　　　　　　　思，故用在肯定句型。在此是用來連接二個動詞，
　　　　　　　即 drive a car 和 ride a bike。

　　* drive〔draɪv〕v. 開（車）　　　ride〔raɪd〕v. 騎
　　　bike〔baɪk〕n. 腳踏車（= bicycle）

14. Did _____?

go to / Mary and John / alone / the park

　　重點結構：問句基本結構

　　　解　答：Did Mary and John go to the park alone?

　　句型分析：Did + 主詞 + 動詞 + 副詞 ?

　　　說　明：助動詞後面放主詞 Mary and John，再接動詞 go
　　　　　　　to the park，alone 為副詞，修飾動詞，放在動詞後。

　　* park〔pɑrk〕n. 公園　　　alone〔ə'lon〕adv. 單獨地

15. We won't be able to see _____.

electricity / there is / no / if

　　重點結構：if 條件句

　　　解　答：We won't be able to see if there is no electricity.

　　　句型分析：主詞 + 助動詞否定 + be able to + 原形動詞 + if +
　　　　　　　　there is + 名詞

　　　說　明：We won't be able to see 為主要子句，連接詞 if
　　　　　　　引導表「條件」的副詞子句，而表示「(沒)有…」
　　　　　　　要用「there is (no) + 名詞」，故條件子句應寫成
　　　　　　　if there is no electricity，本題的意思為「如果沒
　　　　　　　有電，我們就無法看見」。

　　* electricity ( ɪ,lɛk'trɪsətɪ ) *n.* 電

## 第二部份：段落寫作

### 【作文範例】

　　Wendy was waiting for her boyfriend in the park
*yesterday*. Her boyfriend, Tim, wanted to surprise her. He
grabbed Wendy from behind and covered her eyes. Wendy
was very scared. She called for help. She hit the man who
was holding her. Finally, Tim let go of Wendy. She turned
around and saw that the attacker was her boyfriend. She
apologized to Tim for hurting him.

　　* *wait for* 等待　　boyfriend ('bɔɪ,frɛnd ) *n.* 男朋友
　　surprise ( sə'praɪz ) *v.* 使驚訝　　grab ( græb ) *v.* 抓住
　　*from behind* 從後面　　cover ('kʌvɚ ) *v.* 遮住
　　scared ( skɛrd ) *adj.* 害怕的　　help ( hɛlp ) *n.* 幫助；求助
　　*call for help* 求救　　hit ( hɪt ) *v.* 打　　hold ( hold ) *v.* 抱著
　　finally ('faɪnlɪ ) *adv.* 最後；終於　　*let go of* 放開
　　*turn around* 回頭　　attacker ( ə'tækɚ ) *n.* 攻擊者
　　apologize ( ə'palə,dʒaɪz ) *v.* 道歉　　hurt ( hɝt ) *v.* 傷害

# 口說能力測驗詳解

＊請在 15 秒內完成並唸出下列自我介紹的句子，請開始：

My seat number is （複試座位號碼）, and my test number is （初試准考證號碼）.

## I. 複誦

共五題。題目不印在試題上，由耳機播出，每題播出兩次，兩次之間大約有一到二秒的間隔。聽完兩次後，請馬上複誦一次。

1. I gave him my pencil.　我給他我的鉛筆。

2. You should ask him for help.　你應該請他幫忙。

3. I came here by bus.　我搭公車來這裡。

4. Today is the tenth of December.　今天是十二月十日。

5. No, it's not raining now.　不，現在沒有在下雨。

【註】 give〔gɪv〕v. 給　　pencil〔'pɛnsl〕n. 鉛筆
help〔hɛlp〕n. 幫忙
*ask sb. for help* 請某人幫忙
by〔baɪ〕prep. 搭（交通工具）
tenth〔tɛnθ〕n. （每月的）十日
December〔dɪ'sɛmbɚ〕n. 十二月
rain〔ren〕v. 下雨

## II. 朗讀句子與短文

共有五個句子及一篇短文，請先利用一分鐘的時間閱讀試題上
的句子與短文，然後在一分鐘內以正常的速度，清楚正確的朗
讀一遍。

**One** : I'll go to the market to buy some fruit.
我將要去市場買些水果。

**Two** : That test was the hardest one yet.
那個測驗是目前爲止最難的。

**Three** : Is that order for here or to go?
請問餐點是要內用還是帶走？

**Four** : It usually rains a lot in April.
四月通常會下很多雨。

**Five** : I met a very interesting man at John's party
yesterday.
我昨天在約翰的派對上遇到一個很有趣的男人。

【註】 market ('markɪt ) *n.* 市場　　fruit ( frut ) *n.* 水果
test ( tɛst ) *n.* 測驗　　hard ( hɑrd ) *adj.* 困難的
yet ( jɛt ) *adv.* 到目前爲止　　order ('ɔrdɚ ) *n.* 餐點
*for here or to go* 內用還是外帶
usually ('juʒʊəlɪ ) *adv.* 通常　　*a lot* 許多
April ('eprəl ) *n.* 四月　　meet ( mit ) *v.* 遇見
interesting ('ɪntrɪstɪŋ ) *adj.* 有趣的
party ('pɑrtɪ ) *n.* 派對

Six : My favorite hobby is swimming. I learned to swim when I was very young, so I've always been comfortable in the water. I usually swim at the public pool down the street. It's never too crowded and it's not expensive. Next year, I plan to join the swim team at my high school. I hope I'm good enough to make it!

我最喜愛的嗜好是游泳。我在很小的時候就學游泳，所以我在水中總是很自在。我通常在街道另一頭的公共游泳池游泳。它絕不會太擁擠，也不會太貴。明年，我計畫要參加我高中的游泳隊。我希望我的泳技夠好，能夠成功地加入游泳隊！

【註】 favorite〔'fevərɪt〕adj. 最喜愛的
hobby〔'hɑbɪ〕n. 嗜好　　swim〔swɪm〕v. n. 游泳
learn〔lɜn〕v. 學習　　young〔jʌŋ〕adj. 年輕的
always〔'ɔlwez〕adv. 總是
comfortable〔'kʌmfətəbḷ〕adj. 舒適的；自在的
public〔'pʌblɪk〕adj. 公共的
pool〔pul〕n. 游泳池（= swimming pool）
street〔strit〕n. 街道　　down the street 在街道的那一邊
never〔'nɛvə〕adv. 從未　　crowded〔'kraʊdɪd〕adj. 擁擠的
expensive〔ɪk'spɛnsɪv〕adj. 昂貴的　　next year 明年
plan〔plæn〕v. 計畫　　join〔dʒɔɪn〕v. 參加
team〔tim〕n. 隊　　swim team 游泳隊
high school 高中　　hope〔hop〕v. 希望
enough〔ə'nʌf〕adv. 足夠地　　make it 成功；辦到

## III. 回答問題

共七題。題目不印在試題上，由耳機播出，每題播出兩次，兩次之間大約有一到二秒的間隔。聽完兩次後，請馬上回答，每題回答時間爲 15 秒，請在作答時間内儘量的表達。

**1. Q** : You left your book bag on a city bus. You go to the Lost and Found office. What do you say to the person there?

你把你的書包忘在市區公車上。你前往失物招領處。你會跟那裡的人說些什麼？

**A1** : I would say, "Hello. I'm looking for a book bag. It's blue with green trim. Has anyone turned in a bag like that?"

我會說：「哈囉。我在找一個書包。它是藍色鑲綠邊的。有任何人拿像那個樣子的書包來嗎？」

【註】 leave〔liv〕v. 遺留　　***book bag*** 書包
city〔'sɪtɪ〕n. 都市　　***city bus*** 市區公車
lost〔lɔst〕adj. 遺失的　　find〔faɪnd〕v. 找到
office〔'ɔfɪs〕n. 辦公室
***Lost and Found office*** 失物招領處
person〔'pɝsn̩〕n. 人　　hello〔hə'lo〕interj. 哈囉
***look for*** 尋找　　blue〔blu〕adj. 藍色的
green〔grin〕adj. 綠色的　　trim〔trɪm〕n. 鑲邊飾
***turn in*** 交回；交出　　like〔laɪk〕prep. 像

**A2**：I would say, "Excuse me. I left my bag on bus number 32 yesterday. It's red and is filled with books. Do you have it?"

我會說：「不好意思。我昨天把書包忘在 32 號公車上。它是紅色的，而且裝滿了書。你們這裡有嗎？」

**A3**：I would say, "Hi. I lost a bag on one of your buses. It's quite important to me. Would you mind checking to see if you have it?"

我會說：「嗨。我把書包忘在你們的公車上。它對我來說很重要。你介意幫我查查你們這裡有嗎？」

〰〰〰〰〰〰〰〰〰

**2. Q**：You order some food in a restaurant. When it arrives, you find that the meat is undercooked. What do you do? 你在餐廳裡點了一些食物。當食物送來時，你發現肉沒煮熟。你會怎麼做？

【註】　number (ˈnʌmbɚ) *n.* 第…號　　red ( rɛd ) *adj.* 紅色的
　　　**be filled with** 裝滿了　　hi ( haɪ ) *interj.* 嗨
　　　quite ( kwaɪt ) *adv.* 相當
　　　important ( ɪmˈpɔrtn̩t ) *adj.* 重要的
　　　mind ( maɪnd ) *v.* 介意　　check ( tʃɛk ) *v.* 檢查；確認
　　　if ( ɪf ) *conj.* 是否　　order (ˈɔrdɚ ) *v.* 點 ( 餐 )
　　　food ( fud ) *n.* 食物　　restaurant (ˈrɛstərənt ) *n.* 餐廳
　　　arrive ( əˈraɪv ) *v.* 送達　　find ( faɪnd ) *v.* 發現
　　　meat ( mit ) *n.* 肉
　　　undercooked (ˈʌndɚˌkʊkt ) *adj.* 尚未煮熟的

**A1**: I would call the waiter. I would tell him about
the problem and I would ask him to take the dish
back to the kitchen. I would ask him to bring me
another one as soon as possible.

我會叫服務生過來。我會告訴他這個問題，然後會請
他把菜端回廚房。我會要求他儘快再送另一份過來。

**A2**: I would complain to the waiter or the manager.
I would ask them to cook it again. If they said no,
I would leave the restaurant.

我會跟服務生或經理抱怨。我會要求他們再煮一次。
如果他們說不，我會離開餐廳。

【註】 call〔kɔl〕v. 叫；請…來
　　　 waiter〔'wetɚ〕n. 服務生
　　　 ***tell sb. about sth.*** 告訴某人關於某事
　　　 problem〔'prɑbləm〕n. 問題　　ask〔æsk〕v. 要求
　　　 ***take sth. back to*** 把某物拿回…
　　　 dish〔dɪʃ〕n. 菜餚　　kitchen〔'kɪtʃɪn〕n. 廚房
　　　 bring〔brɪŋ〕v. 帶來
　　　 another〔ə'nʌðɚ〕adj. 另一個的
　　　 ***as soon as possible*** 儘快
　　　 complain〔kəm'plen〕v. 抱怨
　　　 manager〔'mænɪdʒɚ〕n. 經理　　cook〔kʊk〕v. 煮
　　　 again〔ə'gɛn〕adv. 再一次　　leave〔liv〕v. 離開

**A3**：I would probably send it back and then order something different. Otherwise, they might just give me the same food again. It wouldn't taste right.
我可能會把它退回去，然後點其他不同的東西。否則，他們可能只是再給我同樣的食物。嚐起來不會好吃。

---

**3. Q**：You are shopping in a big mall. You need to go to the restroom, but you cannot find one. What would you do? 你正在大型購物中心購物。你需要去廁所，但是你找不到。你會怎麼做？

**A1**：I would go into a store and ask a clerk. I would say, "Excuse me. Is there a restroom near here? Can you point me in the right direction?"
我會走進一間商店，然後問店員。我會說：「不好意思。這附近有廁所嗎？可以請你爲我指出正確的方向嗎？」

【註】 probably (ˈprɑbəblɪ) adv. 可能
**send** sth. **back** 把某物送回去
different (ˈdɪfrənt) adj. 不同的
otherwise (ˈʌðə͵waɪz) adv. 否則　　just (dʒʌst) adv. 只
same (sem) adj. 同樣的　　taste (test) v. 嚐起來
right (raɪt) adj. 好的；正確的　　shop (ʃɑp) v. 購物
mall (mɔl) n. 購物中心
restroom (ˈrɛst͵rum) n. 廁所 (= rest room)
**go into** 進入　　store (stor) n. 商店
clerk (klɜk) n. 店員　　near (nɪr) prep. 在…附近
point (pɔɪnt) v. 指給 (某人)
direction (dəˈrɛkʃən) n. 方向

**A2**：I would look for a map of the mall. They usually mark the restrooms. Then I would find one on my own.

我會找一份購物中心的地圖。它們通常會標示出廁所。然後我會自己找。

**A3**：I would find a worker who wasn't too busy. Then I would ask for directions. I'm sure they get asked that kind of question all the time.

我會找一個不太忙的工作人員。然後我會請他給我指示。我確定他們常常被問到那樣的問題。

---

**4. Q**：You are visiting your friend at his or her house and you break a glass. What do you say to your friend?

你正在朋友家拜訪，而且你打破了一個玻璃杯。你會跟你的朋友說什麼？

【註】 map〔mæp〕n. 地圖　usually〔'juʒʊəlɪ〕adv. 通常
mark〔mɑrk〕v. 標示　**on one's own** 獨力；靠自己
worker〔'wɜkɚ〕n. 工作人員
busy〔'bɪzɪ〕adj. 忙碌的　**ask for** 要求
sure〔ʃʊr〕adj. 確定的　kind〔kaɪnd〕n. 種類
question〔'kwɛstʃən〕n. 問題
**all the time** 時常　visit〔'vɪzɪt〕v. 拜訪
break〔brek〕v. 打破　glass〔glæs〕n. 玻璃杯；玻璃

**A1**：I would say, "Uh, oh.　I just broke a glass.　I'm really sorry.　I hope it wasn't expensive."

我會說：「嗯，喔。我剛剛打破了一個玻璃杯。我真的很抱歉。我希望它不是很貴。」

**A2**：I would say, "Oh, no!　I broke your glass.　I'm so sorry.　Please let me replace it."

我會說：「喔，怎麼會這樣！我打破了你的玻璃杯。我很抱歉。請讓我賠償它。」

**A3**：I would say, "Watch out!　I just broke a glass.　There might be some sharp glass on the floor.　Let me clean it up."

我會說：「小心！我剛剛打破一個玻璃杯。地上可能會有一些尖銳的玻璃。讓我來把它清理乾淨。」

---

**5. Q**：You are meeting a friend at the train station.　Her train is late and has not arrived yet.　How would you find out what happened?

你要在火車站接一個朋友。她的火車誤點了，而且還沒抵達。你會如何查出發生了什麼事？

【註】 uh〔ʌ〕*interj* 啊　　oh〔o〕*interj* 喔
　　　*Oh, no!* 哦，怎麼會！　　replace〔rɪˈples〕*v.* 取代；賠還
　　　*Watch out!* 小心！　　just〔dʒʌst〕*adv.* 剛剛
　　　sharp〔ʃɑrp〕*adj.* 銳利的　　floor〔flor〕*n.* 地板
　　　*clean up* 清理乾淨　　meet〔mit〕*v.* 接（某人）
　　　*train station* 火車站　　late〔let〕*adj.* 遲的
　　　arrive〔əˈraɪv〕*v.* 到達　　*not…yet* 尚未…
　　　*find out* 查出；找出　　happen〔ˈhæpən〕*v.* 發生

A1：I would go to the information desk. I would ask if the train had been delayed. Most importantly, I would find out what time it was expected to arrive.

我會到服務台去。我會詢問火車是否被延誤。最重要的是，我會查出火車預計什麼時候抵達。

A2：I would look at the arrivals schedule. It will usually say if a train is on time or delayed. If it is delayed, it will also give the new arrival time.

我會查看火車到站時刻表。它通常會顯示火車是否準點或誤點。如果火車誤點的話，它也會顯示新的抵達時間。

A3：I would ask one of the workers in the train station. I would say, "Excuse me. I'm waiting for the 9:00 train from Taipei. It hasn't arrived yet. Do you know what happened?" 我會詢問一位火車站的工作人員。我會說：「不好意思。我在等一輛九點從台北出發的火車。它尚未抵達。你知道發生了什麼事嗎？」

【註】 information〔͵ɪnfəˈmeʃən〕 n. 訊息
　　　 desk〔dɛsk〕 n. 櫃台　　　**information desk** 服務台
　　　 delay〔dɪˈle〕 v. 延遲；延誤
　　　 importantly〔ɪmˈpɔrtn̩tlɪ〕 adv. 重要地
　　　 **most importantly** 最重要的是
　　　 expect〔ɪkˈspɛkt〕 v. 預期　　　***look at*** 看一看
　　　 arrival〔əˈraɪvl̩〕 n. 抵達
　　　 schedule〔ˈskɛdʒul〕 n. 時間表　　　say〔se〕 v. 寫著
　　　 ***on time*** 準時　　　give〔gɪv〕 v. 提供
　　　 ***wait for*** 等待　　　Taipei〔ˈtaɪˈpe〕 n. 台北

**6. Q** ： You see your friend taking a walk with her new baby.  It's the first time you have seen the baby.  What do you say?  你看見你的朋友正帶著她的新生兒一起散步。這是你第一次看見那個嬰兒。你會說些什麼？

**A1** : I would say, "Oh, what an angel!  She looks just like you!  You're so lucky to have a healthy and beautiful baby."

我會說：「喔，眞是一位天使！她長得眞像妳！你眞幸運，能夠擁有一個健康又漂亮的寶寶。」

**A2** : I would say, "What a surprise!  I didn't expect to meet you here.  May I look at the baby?  Oh, he's gorgeous."  我會說：「眞令人驚喜！我沒想到會在這裡遇見你。我可以看看小寶寶嗎？喔，他眞漂亮。」

**A3** : I would say, "So this is your new son!  He's so sweet!  You must be very proud."  我會說：「這是你剛出生的兒子喔！他眞可愛！你一定很驕傲。」

【註】　*take a walk* 散步　　new〔nju〕*adj.* 新生的；新近出現的
baby〔'bebɪ〕*n.* 嬰兒　　*the first time* 第一次
angel〔'endʒəl〕*n.* 天使　　*look like* 看起來像
lucky〔'lʌkɪ〕*adj.* 幸運的　　healthy〔'hɛlθɪ〕*adj.* 健康的
beautiful〔'bjutəfəl〕*adj.* 美麗的
surprise〔sə'praɪz〕*n.* 驚喜
gorgeous〔'gɔrdʒəs〕*adj.* 非常漂亮的
son〔sʌn〕*n.* 兒子　　sweet〔swit〕*adj.* 可愛的
proud〔praʊd〕*adj.* 驕傲的

**7. Q** : You want to play tennis this afternoon. How would you invite someone to play with you?

你今天下午想打網球。你要如何邀請某人來跟你打？

**A1** : I would say, "How about a game of tennis? It would be fun and we could also get some exercise. We could play about 3:00." 我會說：「來場網球比賽如何？它會很有趣，而且我們也可以順便做點運動。我們可以在三點左右打。」

**A2** : I would say, "Are you free this afternoon? Do you want to play tennis with me? It would be just for fun." 我會說：「你今天下午有空嗎？你想要跟我打網球嗎？純粹是打好玩的。」

**A3** : I would say, "Let's play tennis this afternoon. You're such a good player. I think I can learn a lot from you." 我會說：「我們今天下午來打網球吧。你是個高手。我想我可以從你那裡學到很多東西。」

【註】 play〔ple〕v. 打（球）　　tennis〔'tɛnɪs〕n. 網球
invite〔ɪn'vaɪt〕v. 邀請　　***How about~?*** ～如何？
game〔gem〕n. 比賽　　fun〔fʌn〕adj. 有趣的
exercise〔'ɛksɚ͵saɪz〕n. 運動　　free〔fri〕adj. 有空的
***for fun*** 為了好玩　　such〔sʌtʃ〕adj. 如此的
player〔'pleɚ〕n. 選手

＊請將下列自我介紹的句子再唸一遍，請開始：

My seat number is （複試座位號碼）, and my test number is （初試准考證號碼）.

附錄

# 全民英語能力分級檢定測驗簡介

「全民英語能力分級檢定測驗」(General English Proficiency Test)，簡稱「全民英檢」（GEPT），旨在提供我國各階段英語學習者一套公平、有效且可靠之英語能力評量工具，測驗對象包括在校學生及一般社會人士，可做為學習成果檢定、教學改進及公民營機構甄選人才等之參考。

本測驗為標準參照測驗（criterion-referenced test），參考我國英語教育體制，制定分級標準，整套系統共分五級——初級（Elementary）、中級（Intermediate）、中高級（High-Intermediate）、高級（Advanced）、優級（Superior）。每級訂有明確能力標準，報考者可依英語能力選擇適當級數報考，每級均包含聽、說、讀、寫四項完整的測驗，通過所報考級數的能力標準即可取得該級的合格證書。

# 初級英語能力測驗簡介

## I. 通過初級檢定者的英語能力

| 聽 | 讀 | 寫 | 說 |
|---|---|---|---|
| 能聽懂與日常生活相關的淺易談話，包括價格、時間及地點等。 | 可看懂與日常生活相關的淺易英文，並能閱讀路標、交通標誌、招牌、簡單菜單、時刻表及賀卡等。 | 能寫簡單的句子及段落，如寫明信片、便條、賀卡及填表格等。對一般日常生活相關的事物，能以簡短的文字敘述或說明。 | 能朗讀簡易文章、簡單地自我介紹，對熟悉的話題能以簡易英語對答，如問候、購物、問路等。 |

## II. 測驗項目

| | 初　試 | | 複　試 | |
|---|---|---|---|---|
| 測驗項目 | 聽力測驗 | 閱讀能力測驗 | 寫作能力測驗 | 口說能力測驗 |
| 總題數 | 30 題 | 35 題 | 16 題 | 18 題 |
| 作答時間 | 約 20 分鐘 | 35 分鐘 | 40 分鐘 | 約 10 分鐘 |
| 測驗內容 | 看圖辨義<br>問答<br>簡短對話<br>短文聽解 | 詞彙和結構<br>段落填空<br>閱讀理解 | 單句寫作<br>段落寫作 | 複誦<br>朗讀句子與短文<br>回答問題 |
| 總測驗時間<br>（含試前、<br>試後說明） | 兩項一共約需 1.5 小時 | | 約需 1 小時 | 約需 1 小時 |

　　聽力及閱讀能力測驗成績採標準計分方式，60 分為平均數，滿分 120 分。寫作及口說能力測驗成績採整體式評分，使用級分制，分為 0～5 級分，再轉換成百分制。各項成績通過標準如下：

## III. 成績計算及通過標準

| 初試 | 通過標準 | 滿分 | 複試 | 通過標準 | 滿分 |
|---|---|---|---|---|---|
| 聽力測驗<br>閱讀能力測驗 | 兩項測驗成績總和達 160 分，且其中任一項成績不低於 72 分。（自 97 年起生效，不溯及既往） | 120<br><br>120 | 寫作能力測驗<br>口說能力測驗 | 70<br>80 | 100<br>100 |

## Ⅳ. 寫作能力測驗級分説明

### 第一部份：單句寫作級分説明

| 級　分 | 説　　　　　　　明 |
|---|---|
| 2 | 正確無誤。 |
| 1 | 有誤，但重點結構正確。 |
| 0 | 錯誤過多、未答、等同未答。 |

### 第二部份：段落寫作級分説明

| 級　分 | 説　　　　　　　明 |
|---|---|
| 5 | 正確表達題目之要求；文法、用字等幾乎無誤。 |
| 4 | 大致正確表達題目之要求；文法、用字等有誤，但不影響讀者之理解。 |
| 3 | 大致回答題目之要求，但未能完全達意；文法、用字等有誤，稍影響讀者之理解。 |
| 2 | 部份回答題目之要求，表達上有令人不解／誤解之處；文法、用字等皆有誤，讀者須耐心解讀。 |
| 1 | 僅回答1個問題或重點；文法、用字等錯誤過多，嚴重影響讀者之理解。 |
| 0 | 未答、等同未答。 |

## Ⅴ. 口説能力測驗級分説明

**評分項目（一）：發音、語調和流利度（就第一、二、三部分之整體表現評分）**

| 級　分 | 説　　　　　　　明 |
|---|---|
| 5 | 發音、語調正確、自然，表達流利，無礙溝通。 |
| 4 | 發音、語調大致正確、自然，雖然有錯但不妨礙聽者的了解。表達尚稱流利，無礙溝通。 |
| 3 | 發音、語調時有錯誤，但仍可理解。說話速度較慢，時有停頓，但仍可溝通。 |
| 2 | 發音、語調常有錯誤，影響聽者的理解。說話速度慢，時常停頓，影響表達。 |
| 1 | 發音、語調錯誤甚多，不當停頓甚多，聽者難以理解。 |
| 0 | 未答或等同未答。 |

**評分項目** (二)：文法、字彙之正確性和適切性 ( 就第三部分之表現評分 )

| 級　分 | 説　　　　　明 |
|:---:|:---|
| 5 | 表達內容符合題目要求，能大致掌握基本語法及字彙。 |
| 4 | 表達內容大致符合題目要求，基本語法及字彙大致正確，但尚未能自在應用。 |
| 3 | 表達內容多不可解，語法常有錯誤，且字彙有限，因而阻礙表達。 |
| 2 | 表達內容難解，語法錯誤多，語句多呈片段，不當停頓甚多，字彙不足，表達費力。 |
| 1 | 幾乎無句型語法可言，字彙嚴重不足，難以表達。 |
| 0 | 未答或等同未答。 |

發音、語調和流利度部分根據第一、二、三部分之整體表現評分，文法、字彙則僅根據第三部分之表現評分，兩項仍分別給 0～5 級分，各佔 50%。

凡應考且合乎規定者，無論成績通過與否一律發給成績單。初試及複試皆通過者，發給合格證書。成績紀錄自測驗日期起由本中心保存 2 年。

初試通過者，可於一年內單獨報考複試，得重複報考。惟複試一旦通過，即不得再報考。

已通過本英檢測驗某一級數並取得合格證書者，自複試測驗日期起 1 年內不得再報考同級數或較低級數之測驗。違反本規定報考者，其應試資格將被取消。

( 以上資料取自「全民英檢學習網站」http://www.gept.org.tw )

# 劉毅英文家教班成績優異同學獎學金排行榜

| 姓 名 | 學 校 | 總金額 | 姓 名 | 學 校 | 總金額 | 姓 名 | 學 校 | 總金額 |
|---|---|---|---|---|---|---|---|---|
| 謝家綺 | 板橋高中 | 40600 | 陳亭如 | 北一女中 | 10400 | 吳秉學 | 師大附中 | 5700 |
| 王芓蓁 | 北一女中 | 36850 | 鄭涴心 | 板橋高中 | 10100 | 蔡承紜 | 景美女中 | 5600 |
| 吳書軒 | 成功高中 | 36100 | 何思瑩 | 和平高中 | 10000 | 王凱弘 | 師大附中 | 5600 |
| 趙啓鈞 | 松山高中 | 34650 | 暹定鴻 | 格致高中 | 9400 | 翁子惇 | 縣格致中學 | 5500 |
| 袁好蓁 | 武陵高中 | 32850 | 黃靖儒 | 建國中學 | 9300 | 許廷瑋 | 延平高中 | 5400 |
| 林怡廷 | 清華大學 | 27800 | 陳冠儒 | 大同高中 | 9200 | 林原道 | 和平高中 | 5400 |
| 王挺之 | 建國中學 | 27200 | 徐子瑤 | 松山高中 | 9000 | 陳子文 | 成功高中 | 5400 |
| 羅之勵 | 大直高中 | 25900 | 吳易倫 | 板橋高中 | 9000 | 陳姿穎 | 縣格致中學 | 5400 |
| 蕭允惟 | 景美女中 | 25500 | 潘育誠 | 成功高中 | 8800 | 謝承諭 | 建國中學 | 5300 |
| 黃筱雅 | 北一女中 | 25000 | 陳庭偉 | 板橋高中 | 8800 | 戚世旻 | 格致高中 | 5300 |
| 王廷鎧 | 建國中學 | 24400 | 王千瑀 | 景美女中 | 8700 | 謝孟儒 | 百齡高中 | 5300 |
| 許嘉容 | 北市商 | 24400 | 巫冠毅 | 板橋高中 | 8600 | 簡君恬 | 師大附中 | 5100 |
| 潘羽薇 | 丹鳳高中 | 19600 | 黃新雅 | 松山高中 | 8600 | 施昊恩 | 板橋高中 | 5000 |
| 蘇芳萱 | 大同高中 | 19500 | 林承慶 | 建國中學 | 8600 | 周湘承 | 時雨國中 | 5000 |
| 林政頴 | 中崙高中 | 18800 | 謝竣宇 | 建國中學 | 8400 | 周書廷 | 明倫高中 | 4900 |
| 郭學豪 | 和平高中 | 18700 | 江方 | 中山女中 | 8300 | 謝育珊 | 景美女中 | 4800 |
| 邱靜荳 | 縣格致中學 | 18300 | 吳念馨 | 永平高中 | 8200 | 呂昀靜 | 縣格致中學 | 4700 |
| 郭子瑄 | 新店高中 | 17500 | 王舒亭 | 縣格致中學 | 8200 | 林宇嫻 | 板橋高中 | 4700 |
| 柯博軒 | 成功高中 | 17500 | 潘威霖 | 建國中學 | 8100 | 林珈欣 | 格致高中 | 4700 |
| 陳瑾慧 | 北一女中 | 16500 | 吳沛璇 | 靜修女中 | 7900 | 杜懿樺 | 新莊高中 | 4600 |
| 陳聖妮 | 中山女中 | 16400 | 俞欣妍 | 大直高中 | 7900 | 孫廷瑋 | 成功高中 | 4600 |
| 蔡欣儒 | 百齡高中 | 16300 | 林妤靜 | 格致高中 | 7800 | 徐銘聰 | 明德高中 | 4500 |
| 施衍廷 | 成功高中 | 15700 | 楊沐焓 | 師大附中 | 7750 | 林禹辰 | 成功高中 | 4400 |
| 詹皓翔 | 新莊高中 | 15500 | 許瑞庭 | 內湖高中 | 7700 | 黃紹瑋 | 格致高中 | 4400 |
| 廖彥綸 | 師大附中 | 15400 | 高維均 | 麗山高中 | 7700 | 鄭倢安 | 中山女中 | 4300 |
| 何俊毅 | 師大附中 | 14800 | 李承祐 | 成功高中 | 7700 | 楊覆萋 | 格致高中 | 4300 |
| 陳昕 | 麗山高中 | 14600 | 吳蜜妮 | 西松高中 | 7700 | 朱品潔 | 內湖高中 | 4300 |
| 簡士益 | 格致高中 | 14500 | 林冠宏 | 林口高中 | 7600 | 盧姿樺 | 育成高中 | 4200 |
| 宋才闓 | 成功高中 | 14500 | 鄭懿珊 | 北一女中 | 7600 | 張瑜倩 | 明倫高中 | 4200 |
| 王秉立 | 板橋高中 | 14300 | 林育汝 | 中山女中 | 7400 | 陳建豪 | 格致高中 | 4200 |
| 廖崇鈞 | 大同高中 | 13800 | 柯賢鴻 | 松山高中 | 7400 | 羅勻彤 | 北一女中 | 4100 |
| 鄭晴 | 北一女中 | 13800 | 張謦馨 | 板橋高中 | 7300 | 林天佑 | 中崙高中 | 4100 |
| 張馥雅 | 北一女中 | 13700 | 陳冠廷 | 薇閣國小 | 7150 | 林庭瑜 | 新莊高中 | 4100 |
| 方冠予 | 北一女中 | 13500 | 謝瑜容 | 中山女中 | 7100 | 陳建良 | 格致高中 | 4100 |
| 范詠琪 | 中山女中 | 13400 | 郭禹溱 | 北一女中 | 7000 | 許庭軒 | 靜修女中 | 4000 |
| 吳思慧 | 景美女中 | 13300 | 詹羽 | 師大附中 | 6900 | 李文灝 | 西松高中 | 4000 |
| 許瓊中 | 北一女中 | 13100 | 游宗憲 | 竹林高中 | 6800 | 林家慶 | 內湖高工 | 3900 |
| 溫哲興 | 延平高中 | 12200 | 張繼元 | 華江高中 | 6600 | 盧建宇 | 明倫高中 | 3900 |
| 應奇穎 | 建國中學 | 12000 | 張長蓉 | 薇閣高中 | 6500 | 許絜茹 | 大同高中 | 3800 |
| 劉楷坤 | 松山高中 | 11900 | 蘇珞瑄 | 景美女中 | 6400 | 陳千如 | 國三重高中 | 3800 |
| 廖芃軒 | 武陵高中 | 11800 | 黃崇愷 | 成功高中 | 6400 | 洪御哲 | 格致高中 | 3800 |
| 盧昱瑋 | 格致高中 | 11550 | 林建宏 | 成功高中 | 6300 | 高士權 | 建國中學 | 3800 |
| 呂濰雅 | 成功高中 | 11400 | 江婉盈 | 中山女中 | 6100 | 林芳宇 | 成功高中 | 3600 |
| 陳宣蓉 | 中山女中 | 11200 | 林柏翰 | 中正高中 | 6000 | 許芝瑜 | 景美女中 | 3600 |
| 蘇紀如 | 北一女中 | 11100 | 徐詩婷 | 松山高中 | 5900 | 劉映辰 | 中山女中 | 3500 |
| 陳怡靜 | 北一女中 | 11000 | 吳宇珊 | 景美女中 | 5800 | 游紹群 | 成功高中 | 3500 |
| 謝承孝 | 大同高中 | 10900 | 洪珮榕 | 板橋高中 | 5700 | 劉人廣 | 建國中學 | 3500 |

※ 因版面有限，尚有領取高額獎學金同學，無法列出。

# 初級英語寫作口說測驗

主　　　編 / 劉　毅

發　行　所 / 學習出版有限公司　　☎ (02) 2704-5525

郵 撥 帳 號 / 05127272 學習出版社帳戶

登　記　證 / 局版台業 2179 號

印　刷　所 / 裕強彩色印刷有限公司

台 北 門 市 / 台北市許昌街 10 號 2 F　　☎ (02) 2331-4060

台灣總經銷 / 紅螞蟻圖書有限公司　　☎ (02) 2795-3656

美國總經銷 / Evergreen Book Store　　☎ (818) 2813622

本公司網址　www.learnbook.com.tw

電 子 郵 件　learnbook@learnbook.com.tw

書 + MP3 一片售價：新台幣二百八十元正

2015 年 10 月 1 日新修訂

ISBN 978-957-519-993-7